"There's just times I wish I had a mommy, but I can't tell Daddy that."

Jesse's heart constricted. There were times she was sure Nate wished he had a father, but she could never see herself married again. She had been lucky once.

Please, Lord, help me be there for Cindy as I was for Nate. Guide me in the best way to help Cindy.

With her arm still loosely around Cindy's shoulder, Jesse asked, "Does your father have any lady friends?"

"He's always too busy working when he should be resting."

A plan began to materialize in Jesse's mind. "Maybe we can do something about that."

* * *

THE LADIES OF SWEETWATER LAKE:
Like a wedding ring, this circle of friends
is neverending.

GOLD IN THE FIRE (LI #273, October 2004)

A MOTHER FOR CINDY (LI #283, January 2005)

LIGHT IN THE STORM (LI #297, April 2005)

Books by Margaret Daley

Love Inspired

The Power of Love #168
Family for Keeps #183
Sadie's Hero #191
The Courage To Dream #205
What the Heart Knows #236
A Family for Tory #245
*Gold in the Fire #273
*A Mother for Cindy #283

*The Ladies of Sweetwater Lake

MARGARET DALEY

feels she has been blessed. She has been married thirty-three years to her husband, Mike, whom she met in college. He is a terrific support and her best friend. They have one son, Shaun, who married his high school sweetheart in June 2002.

Margaret has been writing for many years and loves to tell a story. When she was a little girl, she would play with her dolls and make up stories about their lives. Now she writes these stories down. She especially enjoys weaving stories about families and how faith in God can sustain a person when things get tough. When she isn't writing, she is fortunate to be a teacher for students with special needs. Margaret has taught for over twenty years and loves working with her students. She has also been a Special Olympics coach and has participated in many sports with her students.

A MOTHER
FOR CINDY

MARGARET DALEY

Steeple
Hill®

Published by Steeple Hill Books™

STEEPLE HILL BOOKS

**Steeple
Hill**®

ISBN 0-373-87293-3

A MOTHER FOR CINDY

Copyright © 2005 by Margaret Daley

Printed in U.S.A.

For I know the plans I have for you,
declares the Lord, plans to prosper you and not to
harm you, plans to give you hope and a future.
Then you will call upon Me and come and
pray to Me and I will listen to you. You will seek
Me and find Me when you seek Me with all your
heart. I will be found by you, declares the Lord,
and will bring you back from captivity.
—*Jeremiah* 29:11–14

Chapter One

Peace at last.

With a deep sigh Jesse Bradshaw sank into the chair at her kitchen table. After the hectic past hour getting her son off to visit his friend Sean O'Brien, she now had time to read her daily verses from the Bible and collect herself before starting her day.

Dear Heavenly Father, please help me to make it through—

Honk! Honk!

Jesse bolted from her chair, nearly toppling it to the tile floor, and raced for the door. Not again. Stepping outside, she scanned her backyard and found that her geese had a large man who was holding a crying little girl, trapped by the edge of the lake. As Jesse hurried toward her pet geese, the one overriding impression was the anger carved into the stranger's face. He tried to shield the child from the irate birds that flapped their wings, hissing and honking their displeasure at their space being invaded.

"Step away from the nest," Jesse shouted across her yard that sloped to the lake behind her house.

"What do you think I've been trying to do?"

The man's anger was momentarily directed at her as she neared him. His dark gaze drilled into her while Fred darted at him and nipped his leg. The stranger winced and held the little girl up higher to keep the geese from attacking her.

"I'll get their attention. You run."

"My pleasure," he agreed between clenched teeth at the same time Ethel took her turn at his other leg.

"Daddy, Daddy, make them go away! I'm scared!" The child hugged her father tighter and curled her legs around him so they weren't a dangling target for the geese.

"Everything's okay, Cindy." He awkwardly patted the child's back while glaring at Jesse, clearly conveying his own displeasure.

"Fred! Ethel!" Jesse put herself between the geese and the man with the little girl. She waved her arms like a windmill and jumped up and down, yelling the pair's names in her sternest voice, hoping none of her neighbors saw this undignified display.

Thankfully Ethel calmed down and waddled toward her nest. Fred, however, would have nothing to do with her. He focused on the stranger, who was trying to back away. Flying around Jesse, Fred went for the man's leg again. Jesse threw herself in front of the goose. She got nipped on the thigh.

"Get out of here," she whispered loudly. Pain spread from the sore place on her leg as she continued to come between Fred and the intruders.

Carrying his daughter, the man hurried across the yard, a limp to his gait. At the edge of her property, he threw a glance over his shoulder, an ashen cast to his dark features. Jesse shivered in the warm spring air. This man was definitely not happy with her geese—or her.

Fred settled down as the two people moved farther away. After giving one final loud honk, he toddled back to Ethel and stood guard, his beady black eyes watching the pair disappear inside the house next door.

So those were her new neighbors, staying in the Millers' summer home.

Jesse headed for her back door, rubbing the reddened area on her thigh. Everyone in Sweetwater knew to stay away from her backyard while Ethel and Fred were guarding their nest. They could be so fierce when their home was invaded.

With all the activity at her own house, she'd forgotten about her new neighbors who'd moved in two days ago. She supposed she should bake them some cookies and welcome them to Sweetwater—oh, and warn them about her geese.

Shaking her head, she stepped into her bright kitchen and came to a stop just inside the door. Her grandfather sat at the table, his gray hair sticking up at odd angles, a scowl on his face.

"Those geese could wake the dead," he muttered into his cup of coffee while taking some sips.

"I'm sorry. I know you went to bed late last night. But someone was in our backyard. You know how they get with strangers."

Her grandfather's head snapped up, and he regarded her with a pinpoint gaze. "Not the Hawthorne boys trying to steal their eggs again?"

"Nope. Our new neighbors." Jesse eased onto the chair next to her grandfather. "And I have to say I don't think I made a very good first impression."

He peered at the clock over the stove. "It's barely eight. Awfully early to be paying us a visit."

"I don't think that's what they were doing."

His bushy dark brows shot up. "What kind of neighbors do we have?"

"Gramps, that's what I intend to find out later this morning."

Several hours later at her neighbor's house, Jesse pressed the bell and waited and waited. When the door finally swung open, she hoisted up the plate of chocolate chip cookies, as though it was a shield of armor, ready to give her welcoming spiel. The words died on her lips.

The man from earlier filled the entrance with his large frame. He wore a sleeveless T-shirt and shorts that revealed muscular legs and arms. Sweat coated his body and ran down his face as he brought a towel up to wipe it away. When her gaze traveled up his length, power came to mind. Her survey came to rest on his face. Her smile of greeting vanished along with any rational thought.

Earlier she hadn't really had time to assess the man who had been partially hidden by his daughter. The impression of anger and the need to get the man and his daughter to safety had been all she had focused on. Now her attention was riveted to him. His rugged features formed a pleasing picture and only confirmed his sense of power—and danger. When she looked into those incredibly dark-brown eyes, she felt lost in a world only occupied by them.

One of his brows arched. "Come to finish me off?"

His deep, raspy voice broke the silence, dragging Jesse away from her thoughts, all centered around him. "No." She swallowed several times. "No, I brought you and your family some cookies." She thrust the plate at his chest, nearly sending her offering toppling to the porch at his feet.

With a step back, he glanced down at the plate of cookies.

"They're chocolate chip," she added, conscious of the fact that he was now staring at her. Not one hint at what was going on in his mind was revealed in his expression. "I wanted to welcome you to Sweetwater—properly."

Finally he smiled, deep creases at the corners of his eyes that glinted. The gesture curled her toes and caused her heart to pound a shade faster. My, what a smile! His wife sure was a lucky woman.

"And earlier wasn't a proper welcome?"

"I'm sorry about not warning you concerning Fred and Ethel. Everyone knows to stay away from my backyard at this time of year. I meant to. But you know how it is. Time got away from me what with the order I needed to fill." Realizing she was babbling, she clamped her mouth closed, trying not to stare at his potent smile that transformed his face.

"Fred and Ethel are pets?"

"I raised Fred after a pack of wild dogs got his mother and father. A friend gave me Ethel for Fred. He really can be a dear."

"A dear? I don't think our definition of *a dear* is the same."

Despite his words, amusement sounded in his voice, and Jesse responded with a grin. "Well, not at this time when he's playing he-goose. You know males and their territory."

The man laughed. "I suppose I do." He took the plate and offered her his hand. "I'm Nick Blackburn and I'm sure my daughter and I will enjoy these cookies."

No wife? Jesse wondered, slipping her hand within his and immediately feeling a warmth flash up her arm from his brief touch. "I'm Jesse Bradshaw. Are you and your daughter going to be here long?"

"Two months."

She remembered the little girl's pale face and plea to her father. "Is your daughter okay?"

"Cindy is happy as a lark now that she's sitting in front of the television set watching her favorite show."

"How old is she? I have a son who just turned eight."

"She'll be seven later this summer." He stepped to the side. "Please come in."

When she'd come over to his house, she'd had no intention of staying. She still had that order to complete. "I'd better not. I can see I interrupted your exercises."

"Your interruption gave me a good reason to call it quits."

Again she looked him up and down, assessing those hard muscles that could only have come from a great deal of work. He had to exercise a lot or his body wouldn't be in such perfect shape. She began to imagine him pumping iron, sweat coating his skin. When she peered into his face, she found him staring at her, and she blushed. She didn't normally go around inspecting men.

"Well, uh," she stammered, searching her mind for something proper to say, "I'd like to say hello to your daughter and explain about Fred and Ethel." Jesse stepped through the threshold into his house. She felt like Daniel going into the lion's den, as though her life were about to change.

"Would you like a cup of coffee or iced tea? I think Boswell made some yesterday."

"I'll take a glass of iced tea if it's not too much trouble."

He gave her a self-mocking grin. "I'm not great in the kitchen, but I believe I can pour some tea."

"Is your wife home?" Boy, that was about as subtle as a Mack truck running someone over.

He turned and headed toward the back of the house, still limping slightly. "No, she died."

"Oh," Jesse murmured, feeling an immediate kinship with her new neighbor. Her husband had been deceased for the past four years and she still missed him.

She followed Nick into the kitchen and stood by the table. He took two glasses from the cabinets and re-trieved a pitcher from the refrigerator. After pouring the tea, he handed her a glass and indicated she take a seat.

He tilted the glass to his mouth and drank deeply of the cold liquid. "This is just what I needed. It's unsea-sonably warm for the end of May."

"Are you from around here?"

"No, Chicago." He massaged his thigh.

"I noticed you're favoring your right leg. I hope Fred or Ethel didn't cause that."

"No. I just overextended myself while exercising. Sometimes I take my physical therapy a step too far." He shrugged. "I guess you can't rush Mother Nature."

Jesse chuckled. "I agree. Some forces have their own time frame."

"Like Fred and Ethel."

"Definitely forces to be reckoned with."

"Yes, I have a few bruises to prove that."

"I really am sorry. As I said earlier, I've been work-ing hard to finish my latest order and before I realized it, two days had passed since you all moved in. I should have come over that first day and warned you."

"Well, consider us warned." Nick sipped some more tea, draining his glass. "Do you want any more?"

Jesse shook her head, realizing she hadn't drunk very much. She watched him go to the refrigerator and refill his glass. He still favored his right leg. "You said some-thing about physical therapy. Did you have an accident?"

A shadow clouded his dark eyes, making them appear almost black. His jaw tightened into a hard line. "Yes."

A naturally curious person, Jesse wanted to pursue the topic, but his clipped answer forbade further discussion. "Are you here for a vacation?" she asked instead.

"Yes." Again a tight thread laced his voice.

"This is a nice place to take a summer vacation. Do you fish?"

"No, never had the time."

"Maybe Gramps can take you and your daughter out fishing one morning. He loves to show off his gear and favorite spots on the lake."

Nick didn't respond. He made his way back to the table and eased down onto the chair across from Jesse. "I'm afraid I've lived in the big city all my life. The great outdoors has never appealed to me."

"Then why did you come to Sweetwater?"

"The Millers are friends of mine. Since they weren't going to use the house this summer they offered it to me. It met my needs."

She opened her mouth to ask what needs but immediately pressed her lips together. Nick Blackburn was a private man who she suspected had opened up more in the past fifteen minutes than he usually did. Whereas anyone meeting her for the first time could glean her whole life history if he wanted. She wouldn't push her luck. Besides, he would be gone in two months.

"Daddy, I'm hungry. When's Boswell gonna be back?" Cindy asked, entering the kitchen. She came to a halt when she saw Jesse sitting at the table with her father. Her eyes widened, fear shining bright in them.

"Don't worry. I left Fred and Ethel at home." Jesse smiled, wanting to wipe the fear from the little girl's expression. "I came over to bring some cookies and to tell you how sorry I am about my geese this morning. When they're guarding their nest, they can be extra mean."

"I just wanted to pet them." Cindy's eyes filled with tears. She stayed by the door.

"They don't like strangers much, especially right now. Maybe later I can introduce you if you want."

Horror flittered across Cindy's face. "No." She backed up against the door.

"That's okay. Do you like animals?"

The little girl hesitated, then nodded.

"Do you have a pet?"

She shook her head.

An uncomfortable silence descended, charging the air as though an electrical storm was approaching. Jesse resisted the urge to hug her arms to her. "Maybe you can come over and meet my son and his dog, Bingo."

"He has a dog?" Cindy relaxed some.

"Yes, a mutt who found us a few summers ago."

"Found you?"

"Or, rather Fred and Ethel. You thought their racket was loud this morning. You should have heard it when Bingo came into the yard. I found him hiding under a bush, his paws covering his face. Of course, you would think that would teach him a lesson. Oh, no. Bingo still tries to play with them. They won't have anything to do with him."

"Not too smart. I've learned my lesson after only one encounter. Stay away from the geese," Nick said with a laugh.

"Actually, Bingo is pretty smart. Nate has taught him a lot of tricks. Maybe you can get Nate to show you, Cindy." Jesse felt drawn to the little girl who seemed lost, unsure of herself.

"Can I, Daddy?"

"Sure, princess."

"Great. Nate will be home later this afternoon. Come on over and I'll introduce you to my son and Bingo. I promise you Bingo is nothing like Fred and Ethel."

"Do you have any other pets?" Cindy took several steps closer.

"I'm afraid I could open my own zoo and charge admission which I probably should since it costs so much to feed them all. Nate has a fish aquarium and a python as well as three gerbils."

"He does!" Cindy's big brown eyes grew round. "He's lucky."

"I don't think he feels that way when he has to feed them. You should hear him complaining."

"I wouldn't mind doing that if I had a pet." Cindy's hopeful gaze skipped to her father.

"Princess, we've talked about this. We live in an apartment. Not the best place for an animal."

Cindy sidestepped to Jesse and whispered so loud anyone in the kitchen could hear, "Daddy's never had a pet. I think one would be good for him. Don't you?"

Nick looked as uncomfortable as the silence had felt

a moment before. He raked his hand through his dark straight hair that was cut moderately short. "I have enough on my plate without having to take care of a pet, too."

"But I'd do that, Daddy."

"Cindy, I don't think we should bore our guest with this."

The firmness in his voice brooked no argument. The little girl's mouth formed a pout, her shoulders sagging forward.

"Well, I'd better be going before Gramps wonders where I disappeared to. Come over after three, Cindy. Nate should be home by then." Jesse stood.

Nick rose, too. "Let me show you to the door."

"That's okay. I know this place well. I often visit when the Millers are here. I'm glad since they're going to be gone this summer that someone is going to be living here. I hate seeing this old house go to waste."

Nick smiled, the gesture reaching deep into his eyes. "Thanks for the cookies. I know I'll appreciate them."

His warm regard sent a shiver up her spine. She backed away. "Welcome to Sweetwater," was all she could suddenly think of to say. Her mind went blank of everything except the man's smile. Before she made a fool of herself, she rushed from the kitchen, relieved he would only be here for a short time.

"I'm sorry Nate couldn't be here this afternoon. He ended up staying at Sean's," Jesse said, running her palm over Bingo's wiry brown hair.

The medium-size dog rubbed himself up against

Cindy, nudging her hand to keep her petting him. "That's okay. Bingo sure is nice."

"Yeah. We were lucky he found us. He has more loving in him than most dogs."

Cindy buried her face against Bingo's fur. "I wish Daddy would let me have a pet. I'd take good care of him."

"I bet you would." Jesse knew of a family down the road whose poodle had puppies a few weeks ago. They would soon be looking for homes for them. Maybe she could convince Nick that a dog would be good for Cindy. A poodle was a small enough dog to live in an apartment. "While you're here, you can play with Bingo any time you want."

"Nate won't mind?"

"Are you kidding? He loves to show off his animals. He wants to be a zookeeper one day."

Forehead creased, Cindy looked at her. "And you don't mind the snake?"

"I have to confess at first it bothered me. But now, I don't mind it. He usually keeps it in its cage. It's only gotten loose once."

"Mommy would have had a fit—" Suddenly the little girl stopped talking and stared down at the sidewalk.

"Snakes, especially big ones, can be scary." Jesse placed her hand on the child's shoulder, wishing she could take her pain away. She remembered having to deal with Nate's feelings after his father had died. She wouldn't have been able to help him as she did if it hadn't been for her faith in the Lord.

"Yes," Cindy mumbled and proceeded to pet Bingo some more, her face still averted.

"How long has your mother been gone?" Jesse asked, her voice roughened with sudden intense emotions.

Cindy lifted her tearful gaze to Jesse's, her lower lip trembling. "About a year. She died in a car wreck. Daddy was in the car, too. He was in the hospital a *long* time." Her voice wavered. "Daddy doesn't like to talk about it."

Jesse drew the child into her arms, stroking her hand down her back. "If you need to talk to someone, I'm a good listener." It had taken Nate a while to open up to her about his father's death, and after he had, he had been much better.

Sniffing, Cindy pulled away. "I'm okay. It's just that sometimes Daddy doesn't know what to do with me, being a girl and all." She swiped her hand across her cheeks and erased the evidence of her tears. "There's just times I wish I had a mommy, but I can't tell Daddy that."

Jesse's heart constricted, making her chest feel tight. There were times she was sure Nate wished he had a father, but she could never see herself married again. Mark had been a wonderful husband, her childhood sweetheart. She could never find another love like they had. She had been lucky once. She couldn't see settling for anything less than the kind of love she had with Mark.

Please, Lord, help me to be there for Cindy as I was for Nate. Guide me in the best way to help Cindy. She's hurting and I want to help her.

With her arm still loosely about Cindy's shoulder, Jesse asked, "Does your father have any lady friends?"

The little girl shook her head. "He's always too busy

working when he should be resting." She glanced toward her house. "That's what he's doing right now. We're supposed to be on vacation, but he's been on the phone for *hours*."

A plan began to materialize in Jesse's mind. "Maybe we can do something about that."

Cindy's eyes brightened. "What?"

"I'll have a party and invite some friends to introduce you all to Sweetwater."

"You will?"

"Yes. How does tomorrow night sound?"

"What about tomorrow night?"

Nick's question surprised Jesse. She hadn't heard him approaching and to look up and see him standing only a few feet from her was unnerving. Her heart kicked into double time. She surged to her feet, smoothing down her jean shorts that suddenly seemed too short.

"Cindy and I were planning a party to welcome you to Sweetwater."

"You don't have to do that."

"I know, but I want to. So pencil me in."

His eyebrow quirked.

"It won't be a large gathering. Just a few people." Jesse heard herself talking a mile a minute. She stopped and took several deep breaths. "How about it? I'm a great cook."

"After tasting your cookies, you won't get an argument from me. They were delicious."

"Yeah, Daddy had half the plate eaten before I even had a chance to eat one."

Jesse laughed. "Then I'll make some more for dessert tomorrow night. My son loves chocolate chip cookies, too. They're a staple around our house."

"But not your husband?" Nick asked, a lazy smile accompanying the question.

"He loved them, too, but he died four years ago. A freak accident. He was struck by lightning." There she went, telling a person more than he asked.

"I'm sorry."

"Daddy, Bingo can do all kinds of tricks. Watch." Cindy stood. "Roll over." After the dog performed that task, she said, "Sit. Shake hands." The little girl took his paw in her hand. "Isn't he terrific? Dogs make good pets."

Nick tried to contain his grin, but it lifted the corners of his mouth. "I'm sure they do, princess."

"Then we can get one?" Cindy turned her hopeful expression on him.

"I'll think about it when we return to Chicago."

"You will?"

"That isn't a yes, young lady. Just a promise to consider it."

Cindy leaned close to Jesse and whispered loudly, "That means we'll get one when Daddy says that."

"I heard that, Cynthia Rebecca Blackburn."

"Oh, I'm in big trouble now. He's using my full name." The little girl giggled and began petting Bingo.

"Would you like to throw the ball for him? He loves to play catch." Jesse retrieved a red ball from the flower bed loaded with multicolored pansies along the front of her house.

"Yes." Cindy moved out into the yard and tossed Bingo's toy toward her yard. The dog chased it down.

"I didn't want to say anything in front of Cindy, but I know where you could get a poodle puppy."

His dark gaze fixed on her. "Thank you for not saying anything in front of Cindy."

"Then you aren't interested?" She heard her disappointment in her voice and grimaced. She never liked fostering her ideas onto another—well, maybe she did. Anyway, pets were good for children and clearly his daughter loved animals.

"I don't know. I—" He looked toward Cindy. "I've never had a dog before. Or any pet for that matter."

For just a few seconds she glimpsed a vulnerability in his expression before he veiled it. "If you decide to get one, I'll help."

"Until we go back to Chicago." A self-mocking grin graced his mouth. "Then, I'm on my own."

"It's not that difficult. Love is the most important ingredient."

"Isn't it always?"

"Yes, it is." She couldn't help wondering where his world-weary tone came from.

He took a deep breath. "I'll think about the puppy. I'll have to consult Boswell, too, since he'll be taking care of the dog."

"Is that the older gentleman I've seen leaving your house?"

"Completely bald?"

"Yeah."

"That's Boswell. I don't know what I'd do without him. He takes care of the everyday details of my life as well as Cindy's."

"Cindy said something about you working this afternoon. What do you do?"

"I'm CEO of Blackburn Industries. We're into a little of everything it seems."

"And you live in an apartment?" she asked without really thinking. Her picture of his home obviously wasn't right.

A sheepish look fell over his features. "I guess it isn't your idea of an apartment. It takes up the top floor of the building I own on the lake in downtown Chicago."

She chuckled. "No. What pops into my mind is maybe four or five rooms at the most."

"Okay, maybe I have space for a pet. I just think dogs should have a yard. All I have is a terrace. Not the same thing."

"If you don't think a dog is a good idea, I know a lady in town who has some kittens she wants to find a home for."

"I get the distinct impression that if I want something, you're the lady to come to."

Jesse warmed under the smile directed at her. The laugh lines at the corners of his eyes deepened and his stance relaxed completely. "I do know what's going on around Sweetwater. If it's to be had, I can probably get it for you."

"I'll keep that in mind."

"A kitten can be a totally indoor animal."

He threw up his hands. "Enough," he said, laughing. "You've convinced me, but I still need to talk with Boswell. Thank you for showing Bingo to Cindy. I haven't seen her smile like that in a while." He turned to leave, then glanced back at her. "You know, I could use a negotiator like you working for my company. If you ever think about moving to Chicago—"

Jesse shook her head, the idea of a big city sending a chill through her. "No, that will never happen. My home is here. I've lived here all my life and can't imagine being anywhere else."

"Oh, well, you can't blame a guy for trying." He started toward his daughter.

"I'll see you at six-thirty tomorrow night."

He stopped and swung back around, a question in his eyes.

"The dinner party. Casual attire. And Cindy is invited, too, as well as Boswell."

Cindy pulled on his arm. "Can we come, Daddy?"

"Sure, princess, if it's not too much trouble." He peered at Jesse.

"No problem. A piece of cake. I throw parties all the time."

Jesse watched the father and daughter walk away. If he only knew about her famous little dinner parties, he might pack up and leave in the dead of night. Tara Cummings would be perfect for him. Cindy needed a mother and Nick needed—well, he seemed awfully lonely. He masked his vulnerability well, but she'd glimpsed it. Besides, any man who worked all the time needed to

"Tara, you're early," Jesse exclaimed when she opened her front door to find her friend standing on the porch.

"I wanted all the juicy details before I meet this man. I heard the Millers weren't coming this summer to Sweetwater Lake. It's your new neighbor, isn't it?"

Jesse turned away from Tara. "I don't know what you're talking about."

"Jesse Bradshaw, we all know when you throw one of these little dinner parties it's to fix someone up. I'm single and recently out of a relationship. Perfect target for your matchmaking."

"I invited Susan Reed tonight, too. You won't be the only one single."

"If we exclude you, I'll be the only single woman here under the age of fifty. Right?"

Jesse slid her gaze away. "Cindy's coming."

"Who's Cindy?"

"My neighbor's almost-seven-year-old daughter."

"I knew it! You're up to your old tricks. Okay, tell me about your new neighbor. I've heard he is dynamite-looking, some kind of millionaire, and besides having a little girl, he has a manservant. He's from Chicago and is only here for a couple of months."

"Where did you hear all that?"

"The usual."

"Susan Reed?"

Tara nodded. "The best source of info in this town. Far better than our newspaper."

"There isn't much else I can add." For some reason she didn't feel right gossiping about Nick. Tara would have to discover for herself how vulnerable he was, how lonely he was, how attractive—*whoa, stop right there, Jesse Bradshaw!* A little inner voice yelled.

"Susan said something about you talking to him yesterday. Is he nice?"

"I wouldn't have invited you if he wasn't."

Tara brushed her long black hair behind her shoulders. "I knew that. I guess I'm a little nervous. Ever since Clint ran out on me, I'm a little gun-shy."

Jesse put an arm around her friend and began walking her toward the kitchen. "Perfectly understandable. Clint will regret his hasty decision one day."

"I just don't understand why he left."

Jesse patted Tara's arm. "Neither do I."

"Do you think he was overwhelmed with the wedding preparations? He kept asking me to elope with him

and end the madness. I should have listened to him."
Tears filled Tara's eyes.

"There, there. You'll forget about him in no time."
Jesse continued to comfort her friend while she glanced
up at the clock over her stove. Fifteen minutes and still
so much to do. "You'll see, tonight will be the beginning of something magical."

Tara pulled back. "You think?"

"You know me. I have a sixth sense when it comes
to matching people up."

Tara gave her a skeptical look. "*You're* the one who
fixed me up with Clint last year."

The heat of embarrassment singed Jesse's cheeks. "We
all fail every once in a while. Just a temporary setback."
She waved her hand in the air. "Look at Maggie and Neil.
They're getting married next month. It all started here one
evening at one of my little dinner parties."

"Don't get me wrong, but they haven't gotten married yet. They had a *loud* argument today at the bank. I
wouldn't be surprised if the wedding was called off."

"They did?"

"Yeah. He was angry about the money she was
spending on the wedding."

The timer on her stove buzzed. Jesse jumped, startled by the sound, but glad for the interruption. She
would check with Maggie tomorrow to see what was
going on. Her reputation was obviously at stake here.
"I'd better get these cookies before they burn."

"Chocolate chip?"

"What other kind is there?" Jesse reached into the

oven at the same time the doorbell chimed. "Can you get that? I have one more batch to stick in, then I'll be in the living room. Just make Nick and his daughter feel at home."

"It could be Susan Reed."

"Nah. Gramps went to pick her up. You know he takes forever."

Tara halted at the entrance into the kitchen. "Is there something going on there that I should know about?"

Jesse laughed. "Could be. They've been friends for a long time and are now finally dating. It's about time that Gramps got involved with someone." *So he will stop meddling in my life,* she added silently.

"*Now* I know why you asked Susan here this evening. You're killing two birds with one stone, so to speak."

The doorbell rang again.

"Go, before my guests decide I'm not home."

"He sure is impatient," Tara grumbled and made her way toward the front door.

While spooning cookie dough onto the baking sheet, Jesse tried to listen to the people in the foyer. It was awfully quiet for a good minute, then she heard Tara's raised voice. Not a good sign. Jesse quickly finished her task and stuck the cookies into the oven.

When a man's voice answered Tara, Jesse knew something had gone wrong. That wasn't Nick speaking. She remembered his voice—how could she forget such a deep, raspy baritone that sent chills down her spine? Hurrying into the living room, Jesse came to an abrupt halt just inside the doorway. Standing toe-to-toe in her house, hands balled at their sides, were Tara and Clint, both furiously whispering to each other.

"Clint, what are you doing here?" Jesse asked, wiping her hands on her sunflower apron. *I didn't invite you,* she silently added, visions of all her hard work that day going up in smoke.

He shot Jesse a narrowed look. "Coming to stop *my* woman from making a mistake."

"I'm having dinner. How can that be a mistake?" Tara's voice rose again. "And I'm not *your* woman. Not since you sped away from my house after calling our wedding off so fast you probably got whiplash."

"We all know why Jesse has these little dinner parties."

The doorbell sounded. Dread trembled through Jesse. Oh great, her guest of honor had finally arrived and World War III was about to erupt in her living room. "Shh, Clint. If you behave yourself, you can stay," Jesse said as she scurried past the couple, smoothing her apron down over her white pants.

"And watch Tara flirt—"

"Clint Clayborne, you heard Jesse. Quiet."

The man thankfully closed his mouth, but the mutinous expression on his face spoke volumes. This wasn't going to be the fun-packed evening she'd envisioned, Jesse thought as she plastered a wide smile on her face and pulled open her front door.

"I'm sorry I'm late, but I got a last-minute call I had to take."

Nick returned her smile with a heartwarming one that quickened her pulse. "That's okay. Gramps isn't back with Susan Reed yet. Come in." Jesse stood to the side to allow Nick, Cindy and an older man, with a completely bald head, to enter. She offered her hand to him. "You must be Boswell."

"Yes. It is a pleasure to meet you, Mrs. Bradshaw."

"Please, Jesse."

She eyed the man dressed in an impeccable black suit, even though it was nearly summer and the dinner was a casual affair. Boswell fit the bill perfectly for a proper English butler with a rich accent, she thought, and she decided her grandfather would have competition for Susan's interest. That might shake things up a bit tonight—not to mention Clint sending her dagger looks every time she glanced his way.

"Mom. I can't find Bingo." Her son came to a screeching halt in the hallway.

"Everyone, I'd like you to meet my son. Nate, this is Cindy, her father, Mr. Blackburn, and Mr. Boswell."

"Just Boswell, madam."

Barking followed by honking permeated the sudden silence. "I think Bingo is out back."

"He knows to stay away from Fred and Ethel." Nate hurried toward the kitchen.

"Please have a seat in the living room. I'd better check on Bingo." Jesse murmured, following her son.

Before she took two steps into the kitchen, the dog shot through the doggie door and raced past her as if monsters were on his tail. She heard one of her geese's familiar honking and realized the dog had narrowly escaped—again.

"I thought he learned his lesson the last time," Jesse muttered as her son rushed after his pet.

"I only have to have one confrontation with those…geese to know not to get within a hundred yards of them."

Jesse jumped, surprised at the sound of Nick's voice behind her. He had come into the kitchen through the dining room and stood framed in the entrance, looking wonderfully handsome in denim jeans and a casual light-blue knit shirt.

"Then you're smarter than Bingo."

"What a relief." He folded his arms across his chest and leaned against the doorjamb, a crooked grin on his face. "Can I help you with anything?"

"With Boswell in your employ, I don't see you asking to help out in the kitchen much."

"I know my way around. I can fend for myself if the need ever arises. Remember, I served you tea yesterday." Nick threw a glance over his shoulder and lowered his voice, "Besides, things are heating up in the living room and I thought I would give—the man and woman some privacy."

"Oh, you must mean Tara and Clint." She'd almost forgotten about them as though Nick's appearance had wiped her mind blank. "Where's Boswell and Cindy?"

"Cindy ran after Bingo and Boswell ran after Cindy."

"They're probably all in Nate's room by now trying to coax the dog out from under the bed. That's where he goes to hide from Fred and Ethel."

"Not a bad idea. Smart dog."

"I've got everything under control."

Nick's brows shot upward.

"The dinner, I mean."

"Are you sure?" He gestured toward the stove.

Jesse whirled about, the scent of burning cookies mocking her words. If she hadn't been so preoccupied with her new neighbor, her senses totally focused on him, she might have remembered she'd had them in the oven or at least smelled something was wrong before it was too late. He had a way of dominating her thoughts. Scary. She was definitely glad he was only going to be here a few months.

Rushing forward, she yanked open the door, smoke billowing out into the kitchen. She coughed, the blast of heat hitting her. Grabbing the hot pads, she pulled out the baking sheet with fifteen toasty, dark-brown chocolate chip cookies on it.

She dumped them in the kitchen sink along with the baking sheet, then turned to find Nick not two feet behind her. Heat scored her cheeks, and she attributed it to the oven temperature bathing her face not seconds before, not to the fact he was so near that she actually could smell his clean, fresh scent with a hint of lime. It vied with the scent of scorched cookies and definitely was a much more pleasant aroma.

"Thankfully that's only one batch of the cookies. Dessert isn't completely ruined." She fought a strong urge to fan herself and instead flipped on the exhaust fan over the stove.

He scanned the kitchen which was neat and clean with little evidence of any meal preparation having taken place. "What are we having tonight?"

"Aren't cookies enough? Granted, I don't have as many as I wanted, but I think each person will have at least three of them."

"A virtual feast. You'll get no protest from Cindy."

"And you?"

He shifted and leaned against the counter, taking his weight off his right leg. "I may need a bit more nourishment."

"Well, in that case, I have a potato salad, hamburgers and baked beans. I thought that would suit the children better. Now that the cookies are done, I'll put the beans in the oven and start the grill." She moved toward the refrigerator and took a casserole dish out.

"Grill them? Out back?"

Jesse peered at him as she placed the beans on the rack in the oven. "Yes."

"With those mon—geese?"

"The grill is on the deck. I thought we would eat out there, too. The evening is lovely. Fred and Ethel won't bother us."

"Weren't they just out on the deck chasing Bingo?"

"No, they always stop short of coming up the steps."

"You couldn't tell from the racket they were making."

"When night comes, they settle down."

"Night isn't for a few more hours."

She straightened, looking him directly in the eyes. "Trust me. You'll be fine."

"I'm not worried about myself, but Cindy was very upset yesterday morning."

"I know, but I want her to feel comfortable over here. Fred and Ethel will stay by the lake and their nest. I promise." She sensed the little girl needed a woman's influence right now in her life. She could never turn her back on a child in need. She intended to befriend Cindy while she was here. "If you want to help, you can bring the tray in the refrigerator out onto the deck while I check to make sure Tara and Clint are all right."

Nick pushed away from the counter. "I haven't heard any sounds from the living room in the past five minutes."

"No, and that has me worried. They were engaged and Clint called it off the other day, just weeks before they were to be married. Claimed he wasn't ready for marriage."

"Smart guy."

Jesse halted at the entrance into the dining room. She remembered Cindy's words about wishing she had a mother. "You don't believe in marriage?"

"It's fine for some people, but I'm not one of them."

The bitterness in his voice caused her heart to ache for the pain he must have endured. What had made him so against marriage? His late wife? Her death? She recalled her own anger after her husband had died. But she was definitely over that. She had been lucky to have one good marriage. The Lord had been good to her and she wanted to share the bounty. She wanted others to have what she'd had.

She escaped into the dining room, warily approaching the living room. She didn't hear any voices. Had they done bodily harm to each other? Clint had been furious that Tara was at one of her little dinner parties. When Jesse stepped into the room, she stopped at the doorway. Clint's arms were wrapped around Tara, his lips locked to hers, their bodies pressed together. The couple didn't even hear her come in nor sense her, so absorbed were they in each other. She was happy for her friend, but now, who was she going to find for Nick? The man needed a good woman to ease the pain in his heart. And Cindy needed a mother.

Deciding she had to rethink her strategy, Jesse started to back out of the living room when Clint and Tara came up for air. Her friend peered over at her and smiled.

"Clint ask me to run off and get married and I said yes." Tara's eyes were bright with happiness. "We're leaving tonight. Not a word to anyone until tomorrow, Jesse."

She held up her hands. "Not a peep out of me. Promise."

Clint threw her a perturbed look. "I should be really mad at you, Jesse, but I guess this dinner you planned knocked some sense into me, so for that reason you'll be welcome in our home." He drew Tara against him. "We need to get moving before Susan gets here."

Tara hurried to Jesse and hugged her. "You know just the right thing to do. What a matchmaker you are! I owe you."

The couple was gone before Jesse could blink. Okay, this was a success. Not quite the one she had planned for the evening, but a match had been made. She would end this evening early and start over tomorrow. There had to be someone for Nick Blackburn, someone special who could change his mind about marriage and give Cindy what she wanted.

His leg ached. Sinking onto a chair on the deck, Nick rubbed it. The two geese were keeping a wary eye on him and he was keeping a wary eye on them out in the yard under a giant maple with a tree house in it and a large sign posted that read, No Girls Alowed. He chuckled at the sign on the ladder leading up to the tree house. What a cool place to escape to and play in. As a boy he would have liked it. But his childhood had been very different from Jesse's son's.

He couldn't believe he was even here this evening. He was doing it for his daughter who had taken a liking to Jesse. She needed a woman's influence in her life and most likely wasn't going to have one when they returned to Chicago in a few months.

Just this morning Cindy asked him about makeup. Six years old! His baby! He had told her she was years—and *years*—away from wearing any. She had wanted to know where her mother's was. That had stopped him cold. He had hated to tell her he'd thrown it out. The look on his daughter's face made him regret doing it in a fit of anger after he'd come home from the hospital that first time.

The throbbing in his leg reinforced his determination to wipe his wife from his memory. The only good thing that had come of their marriage was Cindy, but what was he supposed to do with a little girl? He felt out of his element. He was at home in a boardroom, not playing dolls with his daughter.

He was determined to bond with Cindy one way or another these next couple of months. He owed her that after the past year with him in and out of the hospital having several surgeries on his leg or with him working long hours at his company because of all the time he had been injured. Now at least, he had a good team in place who could run the business while he kept in touch long distance. The only thing he needed to figure out was how he was going to accomplish bonding with his only child.

"I hope you're hungry. I think I prepared enough to feed half of Sweetwater."

Shoving away those memories he usually kept locked up, Nick turned his full attention to the petite woman hurrying across the deck toward him. She reminded him of a breath of fresh air. He liked her straightforward manner, something he wasn't used to in a woman. With his wife he'd never been sure what mood she would be in. Their last year of marriage, all they had done was argue.

"I can probably eat my fair share." He pushed to his feet, ignoring the dull throb that he hadn't managed to massage away.

Favoring his leg, he made his way to the propane grill, ready to assist Jesse. After she lit the grill, she slapped the hamburgers on the metal rack and stood back. He took a deep breath, inhaling her particular scent of jasmine. It teased his senses, reminding him he hadn't been around too many women socially this past year. He wanted to lean close and take another deep breath. He didn't.

Needing some space, he stepped to the railing, his back to her. He stared at the lake, its smooth, blue water having a calming effect on him. "It looks like you have everything under control."

"Yeah. Gramps accuses me of being a control freak. I'm not. Just very organized."

"So am I. I find it's easier to run a company that way."

"And a house." She came to stand next to him.

Her arm brushed against his. He tensed, the feel of her electric. He sidled a step away, a finely honed tension bolting through him. "Where's everyone? Still trying to coax Bingo out from under the bed?"

"I'm sure by now Nate is showing off his animal collection to Cindy and Boswell. Tara and Clint left. And I'm not sure where my grandfather is. He should have been home fifteen minutes—"

The sound of the back door opening interrupted Jesse. She turned at the same time Nick did and ended up touching him again. She shivered from the brief contact. The deck ran the whole length of the house, and they couldn't manage not to brush against each other?

"There you are, Gramps. We were just wondering where you were."

"Susan had something to show me. Lost track of time."

"I'm so glad you could come tonight, Susan." Jesse offered the older woman a bright smile she hoped would cover her sudden nervousness at the nearness of her neighbor. Stepping forward, she made the introductions.

"I wouldn't miss one of your little dinner parties for the world," Susan said as she checked out Nick. "It's so much better to get the latest firsthand."

Jesse blushed, aware that Nick was suddenly staring at her.

"Where's Tara?" Gramps asked, breaking the silence that had followed Susan's declaration.

"She had to leave—with Clint."

"Clint!" Susan exclaimed. "My, my, that does shake things up tonight. What are you going to do, my dear?"

Nick came up behind Jesse and said in a low voice, "Why do I get the feeling I'm missing something here?"

Jesse tried to ignore his question while she thought of an appropriate answer for Susan. "Not a thing. We're going to eat soon and enjoy each other's company. I'm tickled pink that Tara and Clint are back together." Jesse was sure her cheeks were past the pink stage. Cherry-red was more like it.

"You should be. You fixed them up in the first place." Gramps took Susan's hand and led her to the love seat where the tortilla chips and guacamole dip were on a glass table in front of them. He began to munch.

If her grandfather kept his mouth full, maybe she would make it through this evening without Nick realizing she'd planned for him to meet and hopefully date Tara. Of course, there was always Susan, who was a fountain of information and loved spewing it. Jesse was positive that Nick wouldn't appreciate knowing he was part of one of her matchmaking schemes, especially after his earlier comment concerning marriage.

Why was he so against marriage?

"Jesse, dear, I think you should turn the hamburgers." Susan scooped up some dip on a chip and popped it into her mouth.

Caught off guard, Jesse spun about and hurried toward the grill. She flipped the patties over, grimacing when she noticed the slightly charred side. "I really can cook, Nick. I've been distracted this evening. Normally one of my parties goes over without a hitch."

"How often do you entertain?" Nick asked, amusement dancing in his eyes.

"Oh, whenever the urge strikes me." She waved her hand in the air as though to dismiss the subject as unimportant and hoped no one commented.

"I have to admit, this is a beautiful setting for a dinner. I had my doubts about eating outside with those two so near." Nick tossed his head in the direction of the geese now waddling toward the lake. "But you were right. They're staying away."

Fred flapped his wings as though he knew he was being discussed. Jesse chuckled. "You probably shouldn't take a tour of my backyard any time soon."

"You'll have no argument from me."

The back door burst open again, and the children, followed by Boswell, came out onto the deck. Cindy and Nate raced toward them, skidding to a halt a foot in front of them.

Cindy grinned, showing her missing front tooth.

"Daddy, you should see Nate's room. He has so many pets. I got to hold Julia, Rita and Sadie. They're gerbils. Julia went to the bathroom on Boswell."

Jesse swallowed her laugh and tried her best to keep a straight face. Looking at Boswell, she noticed a wet spot on his black suit coat. "I'm sorry. She does that sometimes when she's picked up. Nate should have warned you."

"It must have slipped his mind." Boswell sent a censured look toward Nate.

"It did, Mom. Promise."

"I just came out here to tell you, Mr. Blackburn, that I'm going back to the house to change."

"Sure." Nick, too, was having a hard time keeping his mirth to himself if the gleam glittering in his eyes was any indication.

"Please, begin eating without me. I know the children are hungry."

When Boswell disappeared, Jesse and Nick couldn't contain their laughter any longer. "I wish I could have seen his expression when that happened," Jesse said, wiping the tears from her eyes.

"His face turned real red." Nate grabbed a handful of chips and stuffed them into his mouth.

"I never saw Boswell move so fast." Cindy giggled. "I wanted to play with the animals longer, but Boswell thought we should join the adults."

"Is Boswell a nanny?" Susan asked.

Cindy pulled her father over to the other love seat. "Oh, no. Boswell is a *manservant*," she answered in

a serious tone as though she had been corrected before about Boswell's role and wouldn't make that mistake again.

While Nick and Cindy got to know her family, Jesse
finished the dinner preparations and put the food on the
long picnic table she'd already set earlier. She removed
Tara's place setting, genuinely happy for her friend.
Tara wouldn't have been right for Nick, Jesse decided,
now that she knew him better. Tara was flighty and so
absentminded that she would have driven Nick crazy
after the first date. No, she would have to find someone
more disciplined and in control, more organized.

*God, please help me to find someone for Nick, some-
one to be a good mother for Cindy.*

As she called the others to the table, the perfect match
came to Jesse's mind. Felicia Winters, the lady with the
kittens, and Jesse knew how she could get them together without raising Nick's suspicion with another
dinner party. She smiled as she sat between Gramps and
Nate and across from Nick. She looked right into his
dark eyes and shivered. He was staring at her with an
intense, probing gaze as though he were trying to read
what was going on in her mind. Heavens, she couldn't
have that!

"Do you think Boswell will come back?" Nate asked
after Jesse said the prayer. He bit down on his hamburger, managing to stuff a third of it into his mouth.

"Young man, this isn't a race to see who finishes
first." Jesse passed the baked beans to Gramps.

Her son stopped chewing for a few seconds, then

swallowed his food, making a gulping sound. Jesse rolled her eyes and hoped she didn't run out of patience.

Nate slurped some of his milk, leaving a white mustache on his face. "Sorry, Mom."

She unfolded his napkin and gave it to him. "Please wipe your mouth."

"Jesse, he's doing fine. He's just being a boy."

Jesse resisted the urge to nudge her grandfather in the side to keep him quiet. Instead, she sent him a narrowed look. She loved Gramps, but he wasn't the best role model for her son. Thankfully he wasn't cussing like he used to. When he'd first come to live with them three years before, she remembered having to cover her son's ears on more than one occasion.

"Mr. Blackburn, do you think Boswell will be coming back?" Nate asked again after wiping the napkin across his mouth. Her son took a smaller bite of his hamburger this time.

"He rarely passes up a meal he doesn't have to cook."

"Boswell cooks?" Nate screwed his face into an expression of disbelief. "Gramps wouldn't be caught dead in the kitchen."

"He does more than cook. He takes care of Cindy and me."

A frown creased Nate's forehead. "He's a maid?"

Nick leaned forward. "I wouldn't say that too loud. He doesn't like to be referred to as a maid."

"But that's what he is," Gramps cut in between bites of his baked beans.

This time Jesse did nudge her grandfather in the side.

He grunted. "Well, child, if he cleans up the house, he's doing the work of a maid. If he ain't proud of his job, then he shouldn't do it."

"I'm very proud of my vocation," Boswell said from the steps that led up onto the deck.

Gramps shot him a suspicious glance. "I wouldn't be hanging around down there too long. No telling when Fred will—"

"Gramps! You know Fred isn't that bad. Don't scare Cindy."

Her grandfather mumbled something under his breath and resumed eating.

"I'm not scared," Cindy announced to the silent table of people.

Boswell sat next to Susan Reed and smiled at her as he placed his napkin in his lap. "I must say the aroma coming from here would entice anyone to crash this party."

"I love your British accent. How long have you been in this country?" Susan asked, her whole face lit with a smile.

Gramps muttered something else, just low enough that no one else could hear. Jesse was thinking about stomping on his foot to keep him quiet, but decided nothing would keep her grandfather quiet if he chose otherwise.

"Twenty years."

"Then you're practically an American."

Boswell looked shocked at even the thought of not being considered English. He tightened his mouth while his hand clutched his fork, his knuckles white.

"This is the best—" her grandfather paused, groping for the right words to say with children listening "—country in the world," he interjected in the conversation between Boswell and Susan.

Boswell's face turned beet-red. His knuckles whitened even more around the fork still clenched in his hand.

Jesse knew the Revolutionary War was about to be fought again on her deck. She shot to her feet, her napkin floating to the bench. "Gramps, will you help me with the dessert?"

"I'm not through yet. Besides, what can be so hard about carrying a tray of cookies?"

"I—" She couldn't think of anything to say.

"I'll help you." Nick stood, walked by Boswell and leaned down to whisper something in the man's ear.

Jesse followed Nick into the kitchen. "I don't know if it's wise to leave my grandfather and Boswell out there together. When Gramps gets going—" She let the implied threat trail off into silence.

Nick's chuckle was low. "I believe Boswell can hold his own. I reminded him that Cindy and Nate were listening."

"I wish that would work with my grandfather. He told me when he turned seventy a few years back that he had earned the privilege of speaking his mind whenever he wanted. I've gotten him to tone down his language, but even that was a battle. I love my grandfather, but he isn't always the best male example for my son." She peered out the window at the group left on the deck. "Well, I guess what you said worked. The two men are still seated and I don't hear any shouting."

"That's a good sign."

"I really don't need your help. I was just trying to get Gramps away from the table."

"Really?" One of his dark eyebrows quirked.

"And as usual, it didn't work." Jesse walked to the refrigerator to retrieve the gallon of homemade peach ice cream she and Nate had made earlier that day. "If you want, you can get the bowls from the cabinet and some spoons from that drawer." She gestured toward the one next to the dishwasher.

She slid a glance toward him as he opened the cabinet. They were alone. This was her chance to see about the kitten for Cindy and set her plan in motion for him to meet Felicia. She noticed the sure way he executed his task as though he was very familiar with her kitchen. This man seemed at home anywhere—even when Fred was attacking him yesterday morning. His well-built body—whoa! That wasn't what she was supposed to be doing, ogling her guest, a guest she was planning to fix up with Felicia.

Jesse tore her gaze away from him and asked, "Have you made up your mind about the kitten for Cindy?" There she was back on track with her plan—Felicia and Nick.

Chapter Three

"I don't think I have much choice." Nick placed the bowls and spoons on the counter.

"You always have a choice. I've got a feeling you're never backed into a corner that you don't want to be in." Jesse cradled the ice-cream container against her chest while retrieving the tray of chocolate chip cookies. The cold felt good against her. It seemed to be unusually hot in the kitchen.

"True, especially in business. But this is personal and it involves my daughter. She wants a pet bad. I suppose a kitten is better than a dog, snake or gerbil, and Boswell agreed with me."

"Then you'll get Cindy a kitten?"

"Yes. You said you knew where I could get one."

She nodded. "We can go tomorrow afternoon. I'll call Felicia and arrange it."

Nick opened the back door and let Jesse go first.

"Don't say anything yet to Cindy. I want it to be a surprise. I don't think she would get a wink of sleep if she knew she was going to pick out a kitten tomorrow."

"My lips are sealed." Jesse pressed them together to emphasize her point, but it was hard for her to contain her happiness. Her plan was back on track. Tomorrow he would meet Felicia and be impressed with her knack for organization. Her home was spotless.

Okay, so maybe Felicia was just a little bit too organized and obsessed with having a clean house, Jesse thought. The sound of the sofa cover crunching beneath her when she sat on Felicia's couch punctuated the silence with that declaration. The plastic stuck to the backs of Jesse's legs and made her conscious of her every move.

The simple act of crossing her ankles and smoothing her shorts down drew Nick's attention. One corner of his mouth lifted. For a few seconds his gaze ensnared hers, and she felt as though they were the only two people in the room. His way of drawing a person's focus to him must be a valuable tool in the business world. In her world, it was disconcerting, Jesse decided.

"I'm so tickled you want to give one of my babies a home." Felicia straightened a stack of magazines on the coffee table. The top one sat at a slight angle from the others. Definitely out of place. "I won't give my babies away to just anyone. Thankfully Jesse can vouch for you."

Somehow Felicia managed to cross her legs, the silence from her action indicating a certain degree of grace that Jesse obviously didn't possess or the fact this woman had had a lot of practice sitting on her plastic covers. Jesse wanted to believe it was the latter.

"Have you ever had a pet before?" Felicia asked, cutting into Jesse's musing.

"No, but I'm sure we'll be able to manage," he answered with all the confidence of a man who was used to running a large company.

"You have to do more than just manage. You have to love your pet." One of Felicia's cats curled herself around the woman's leg, purring. She picked up her pet and buried her face in its fur.

"I can do that," Cindy chimed in, bouncing several times in her enthusiasm.

The sound reverberating through the room drew Felicia's look. The "look" would have made anyone freeze, Jesse thought, and she began to reassess her friend's candidacy for Cindy's mother. Glancing about, Jesse wondered if Felicia spent every wakened moment cleaning her house. The thought sent a shiver through Jesse. She hated cleaning her house and avoided it whenever possible.

Maybe she was being too harsh in her judgment of Felicia. After all, the woman loved cats and anyone who was an animal lover must have room in her heart for children. Jesse stood. "Why don't Cindy and I go pick out a kitten while you and Nick work out the details?" Jesse took the little girl's hand and quickly left the living room. Nick and Felicia needed time alone to get to know each other.

The four kittens were out in the sunroom. One was sleeping on the white ceramic tiled floor, two were prowling and the last one was playing with a piece of gold ribbon. The black kitten with a white mark on its forehead batted the ribbon, chasing it around. Cindy laughed and went over to it. It stopped to check the little girl's lacy socks, licking her leg. She laughed again and picked up the kitten. Jesse noticed the cat was a male.

"I want this one. What do you think?" Cindy cuddled him to her face. "Oh, she's so cute."

"It's a male."

"How can you tell?"

Jesse wasn't prepared to go into the facts of life with Cindy. For a second, nothing came to mind. "He's made differently," she blurted out, sweat beading on her upper lip.

"Oh." Cindy seemed to accept that lame reason, hugging the kitten to her. "Let's go show Daddy."

So much for giving Nick and Felicia time to get to know each other. Jesse searched her mind for a delay tactic. "Don't you want to check out the other kittens to make sure he's the one?"

Cindy shook her head. "I know."

Jesse stood for another minute in the middle of the sunroom, before saying, "Then I guess we should show your dad." Hopefully five minutes was long enough for them to strike up a…friendship. Suddenly the idea of a relationship between Nick and Felicia didn't seem right and that thought bothered Jesse.

When she and Cindy entered the living room, silence hung in the air, Nick's expression neutral. Felicia looked as though she were sitting in a dentist's chair waiting for the drill. Jesse plastered a smile on her face, intending to get the conversation going.

Nick shot to his feet. "We'll take good care of the kitten. Are you sure you don't want any money, Miss Winters?"

Miss Winters? Not a good sign.

Felicia straightened, bristling at his suggestion. "No. A good home is all I request, as I told you a few minutes ago, Mr. Blackburn."

Mr. Blackburn? *Definitely* not a good sign.

"I'll take real good care of Oreo," Cindy said, nuzzling the kitten.

At the door Nick stooped to slip on his shoes while Jesse put hers on then held Oreo so Cindy could buckle her sandals. When Felicia had asked them to take off their shoes before coming into her house, Jesse should have realized the meeting would go downhill from that moment. Nick had started to say something but snapped his jaws closed. That hadn't stopped Cindy from blurting out the question they had all wanted to know, "Why?"

"Goodness me. You might get some dirt on my carpet," Felicia had answered.

Well, one good thing came of this visit, Jesse decided as the door closed behind them. Cindy had her kitten. That had to be worth something.

"An interesting woman," Nick commented as they walked to Jesse's car. "I'm surprised she has cats in her house. Won't they track in dirt?"

"Her cats never go out."

"I see."

Jesse doubted it. She really needed to try one more time. "Felicia's very nice and good with animals…well, cats at least."

"I'm sure she is."

"She's the town librarian. Every Saturday she has a story hour for the children. She's quite good at reading to them. Nate loves to go. Maybe Cindy could go with him next Saturday."

"I'll see," he said as though he wasn't certain he wanted his daughter within a hundred yards of the neat freak whose house they were standing in front of, not a blade of grass out of place.

Nick finished his last leg lift and pushed to his feet. Sweat drenched him. Taking a towel and wiping his face and neck, he stared out the picture window that faced Jesse's house. He saw her climb the steps to the deck and enter her kitchen, her movement a graceful extension of her lithe body. With her brown hair cut short and feathered about her face, her large green eyes and ready smile emphasized her pixie look.

He remembered the time he'd seen Jesse right after he'd finished his physical therapy exercises. He couldn't believe it had only been five days ago. She was all Cindy talked about—besides her kitten and her new friend, Nate. Suddenly he seemed surrounded by Jesse and her family. And the last thing he needed or wanted was another woman in his life. He was still piecing his life back together after his accident and his unhappy marriage to Brenda.

He turned away from the picture window and limped toward the door, determined to accomplish two things this summer: get to know his daughter better and get back to being one hundred percent after the last operation on his leg. For two months he'd promised to devote himself to those two tasks. He could run Blackburn Industries from here for that short amount of time. He would have to leave the everyday affairs of his company to his capable staff, but he already had been doing that since the accident. Cindy needed this. He needed this.

"Daddy! Daddy!" Cindy slid to a halt, tears streaming down her face.

He knelt in front of her, the action intensifying the pain in his leg. He ignored it and clasped his daughter's arms. "What's wrong, princess?"

"Oreo's gone!"

Jesse kneaded the dough, flipped it over and started all over again, shoving her palms into it. She pounded her frustration out on the soon-to-be loaf of bread. Still no one came to mind as a possible candidate for Nick and time was running out. He would only be here seven more weeks. Courting a potential wife didn't happen overnight. Of course, it would help if he left his house more often. Then she might have a better chance of fixing him up with someone.

Who? That was the problem. She had been so wrong

about Tara and Felicia. The third one was the charm. But who?

She placed the dough in a blue ceramic mixing bowl and covered it with a damp cloth. The doorbell chimed. She quickly washed her hands, then hurried to answer it.

The worry on Nick's face prompted her to ask, "Is something wrong with Cindy?"

"Yes—I mean, no, not her exactly. Oreo. He's gone. We can't find him and she's beside herself. You haven't seen him, have you?"

"No." She stepped out onto the porch and automatically scanned the area as though that would produce the errant kitten.

"I thought so, but I had to ask. I'm desperate. I promised Cindy I wouldn't come home until I found Oreo. I've been up and down the street, along the lakeshore. Nothing."

"What happened?"

"Oreo darted out the front door when Cindy came back from playing with Nate this morning."

"I'll get Gramps and Nate. We'll come over and make some posters to put up around town. Cindy can help with them. It'll make her feel better if she's doing something."

"When I left, she was in her room crying. She didn't want to talk or do anything."

"I'll get the supplies we need and be right over."

"What should I do in the meantime?"

"Hold Cindy."

"I tried. She cried even louder."

"That's okay. Hold her anyway." Jesse rushed back

into her house to gather some poster board, markers and her family.

When they arrived at Nick's house, Boswell immediately opened the door before Jesse had a chance to ring the bell. Silence greeted her as she entered. She hoped that meant that Cindy had calmed down.

As Boswell closed the door, the little girl, with Nick following, rushed into the foyer, her eyes bright with unshed tears. "You think we'll be able to find Oreo? Daddy said you're gonna help."

The eager hopefulness in the child's voice touched Jesse. She hated making promises she couldn't keep, but it was hard not to say what Cindy wanted to hear. "If Oreo is in Sweetwater, we'll find him."

Heavenly Father, please help me find Oreo. Cindy has already lost a lot in her short life. I know I just made a promise I might not be able to keep. Please help me to keep this one promise.

"What if—"

Jesse laid her hand on the child's shoulder. "No whatifs. That's wasted energy. We need to make some posters to put up around town and then form search teams to scour the area."

"Then let's get going." Cindy took Jesse's hand and dragged her toward the kitchen.

Jesse threw a glance over her shoulder at the rest of the group who remained standing in the foyer. "You heard her. Hop to it."

The children sat on the floor in the kitchen and made posters while the adults used the counter and table.

Cindy copied off Nate and drew a kitten that looked more like a dog.

Nick leaned close to Jesse and whispered, "Do you think this will help?"

Jesse got a whiff of his clean, fresh scent with that hint of lime. Her pulse rate kicked up a notch. This was a rescue mission, nothing more, she reminded herself and said, "I wouldn't be doing it if I didn't. The people in this town are wonderful. When they hear that Oreo is missing, they'll help look, too. This is the best way to get the news out. That and talk to whomever we see while we're putting the posters up."

Doubt reflected in his gaze, Nick went back to work, absently massaging his thigh.

"Is your leg bothering you?"

"Nothing I can't handle."

Jesse wondered about that as she studied the tired lines on his face and the pinched look he wore. He'd already been out looking for the kitten.

"I think it might rain later. I have more trouble when the weather is about to change."

"Then we'd better hurry and get these posters up. We can probably put them in some storefront windows so if it rains it won't matter."

When the group was finished, Cindy wanted to go with Nate and Gramps while Boswell was going to check out the lake area again. Jesse and Nick decided to go in the opposite direction from the children and Gramps. They were all to meet at Harry's Café on Main Street when they were through.

As they started to go their different ways, Cindy said, "Boswell, please don't go near Fred and Ethel."

The older man smiled. "I wouldn't think of it, Miss Cindy."

"Oh." The little girl brought her hand up to cover her mouth, her eyes growing round. "What if Oreo went close to Fred and Ethel? Shouldn't someone check?"

Jesse bent down in front of Cindy. "Believe me. We would have heard a ruckus if Oreo had. But if it will make you feel better, I can check."

The tears returned to Cindy's eyes. "Please."

"Then that's my first stop." She started to stand up.

Cindy tugged on Jesse's arm, stopping her, and whispered in her ear, "Please don't let Daddy get too close. I don't want him hurt again."

A lump jammed in Jesse's throat. "I'll take good care of your father."

"He might not be able to walk very far. His leg's hurting him. It always does after he does his exercises. He'll need to rest, but he'll act like he doesn't."

Surprised at the child's keen observation and assessment of her father, Jesse gave her a reassuring look. "I'll make it seem like it's my idea."

Satisfied that her father would be taken care of, Cindy hurried to Gramps and Nate at the end of the driveway. Boswell took off toward the lake.

Nick came up beside Jesse. "What was that all about?"

"Nothing. Just girl talk."

"Girl talk?" He shook his head. "In the middle of all of this?"

"Let's go. I told Cindy I would check the area by Fred and Ethel's nest first, but you have to stay back."

"Believe me, I didn't have any intentions of going near those two."

Nick followed Jesse around back of her house and waited by the deck while she approached the two geese. They never took their eyes off her, but they remained quiet while she surveyed the area for she wasn't sure what. Everyone would have heard if Oreo had come near Fred and Ethel. But a promise was a promise.

As Jesse made her way back to Nick, his gaze fixed on her and her pulse rate responded as it had earlier. For a few seconds she felt as though they were the only two people in the world. He had a way of stripping away the rest of mankind with merely a look. The intensity in his eyes unnerved her. She wasn't even sure he was aware of it. It cut through defensive layers that protected her heart and was very confounding. When she'd lost Mark she vowed she would never put herself in that position again. The pain of losing her husband had been too much. Sticking to that promise had kept her safe for the past four years.

"All clear," she said, eager to get their search started. There were lots of people in town and suddenly she needed to be around a lot of people. She might even be able to come up with a third candidate for Nick while they looked for Oreo.

As Nick nailed up the posters, Jesse stopped various townspeople to let them know they were looking for a lost kitten, all black except for a patch of white above his eyes. She assessed the women they encountered as possible candidates, but none were suitable.

"Do you know everyone in town?" Nick asked as he hammered another poster to a telephone pole.

"Practically, but then I've lived all my thirty-two years here."

"I've lived all my thirty-five years in Chicago, and I don't know everyone there."

Jesse chuckled. "Not the same thing. A few million more in population can make a difference."

He eyed her. "I'm beginning to wonder with you if it would. Have you ever met a stranger?"

"Sure. You."

Nick favored his right leg more than usual as he walked beside her down the street. He tried not to act as if it were bothering him, but Jesse noticed, had for the past three blocks. That was why she had taken a shortcut to the café. She'd promised Cindy she would look after Nick—whether the man wanted her to or not. And she suspected he would be appalled if he knew what she was thinking.

She stopped in front of Harry's Café. "Let's take a break. The rest of the group should be here soon."

Nick hesitated, surveying the street as if he were checking to make sure every pole had a poster on it.

"It's been a long day. I was up unusually early this morning. I need to refuel. I could use a cup of coffee." She realized six wasn't unusually early in some people's book, but she normally slept until six-thirty so it wasn't a lie. Actually she'd tossed and turned a good part of the night, trying to get her neighbor and his problem out of her brain. She hadn't been very successful so she could use a shot of caffeine to keep going.

Nick opened the door for her and trailed her into the café to a booth along the front window. He slid in across from Jesse, the pinched look about his mouth easing some as he sat. For a few seconds Jesse found herself wanting to soothe away the tired lines about his eyes. She quickly flipped open the menu she knew by heart and studied it.

"I'm starved. I think I'll get a piece of pecan pie, too. They have the best pecan pie in the state here. Goes great with coffee." Jesse was beginning to wonder if Millie, one of the people they had met while passing out posters, had rubbed off on her. First, she was avoiding eye contact with Nick and now she was chattering away nonstop. Next, she would start giggling.

She needed to find a woman for him. Then maybe she wouldn't think about him all the time!

The waitress came over and took their orders. Jesse studied the young woman who was the café owner Rose's niece from Louisville and immediately dismissed her as a candidate. She was too young and, according to her aunt Rose, wild. She wouldn't be a good influence on Cindy.

As the waitress brought them their cups of coffee, the door opened and in walked Beth Coleman. Jesse caught her friend's eye and motioned her to their booth. Beth was quiet, direct and sensible. She was also a very attractive woman with shoulder-length blond hair and sky-blue eyes. She might be just right for Nick. Why hadn't Jesse thought of her before now?

"Beth, it's so good to see you," Jesse said with more enthusiasm than usual.

"We just saw each other yesterday at the grocery store."

Jesse cleared her throat. "I'd like you to meet Nick Blackburn. He's staying in the Millers' house for the summer. Why don't you join us?" She scooted over to give Beth some room to sit.

Her friend hesitated for a few seconds, then took a seat next to Jesse. "I'll join you until Darcy arrives. I needed to talk to you anyway about making one of your dolls for the Fourth of July charity auction at the church. Will you contribute again this year?"

"Of course. I've already started on the doll. I should have it done in a week or so." Jesse looked across at Nick. "Beth's a great organizer. Every year she almost single-handedly puts together a charity auction to benefit the needy families in our area. She also teaches high school English. On the side she teaches art to the young children in the summer. She's quite talented. Beth's so good with children any age." Had she left anything out? Had she made her sound too good to be true? Was she losing her touch as a matchmaker?

Beth blushed a deep scarlet.

"It's nice to meet you. I think I've met half the town today." Nick took a sip of his coffee, a thoughtful expression on his face.

"Jesse's a great one to introduce you around town. I

think she knows more about me than I do. Maybe I should take you along on my next job interview."

Panicked her friend might be leaving town, Jesse said, "Nate has a few years to go before he gets to high school. He's got to have you for English. You aren't looking for another job, are you?"

Beth laughed. "You never know."

Jesse studied her friend for a moment, wondering what she meant by that answer. "Nick has a six-year-old daughter. It might be nice if she joined one of your classes this summer. Nate's taking the art class. It starts next week. What's nice is that the parents can participate with the children."

"I'm a firm believer that parents and children should do a lot of activities together. I have a few openings still in the art class if you're interested, Mr. Blackburn."

"That really will have to be Cindy's choice. I'll talk to her about it."

His gaze narrowed onto Jesse. She tried not to squirm under its intensity, but it was difficult to sit still.

"Just let Jesse know. She can tell you how to sign up your daughter." Beth rose, waving toward someone entering the café. "I see Darcy. I'd better go. We still have a lot of planning to do for the auction. It's only a month away." She hurried toward Darcy Markham.

Jesse ignored Nick—or rather his glare—and watched her best friend from high school fix her gaze on her and Nick in the booth. She could see a surprised expression descend on Darcy's face. Bypassing the table Beth had snagged for them, Darcy headed straight toward Jesse.

"Okay, Jesse Bradshaw, what's going on here?" Nick asked, his deep, raspy voice compelling her to look away from her friend and toward him.

Chapter Four

Jesse wanted to say, "Quick. Hide me," before Darcy reached the table, but instead she found her voice snatched away at the intensity in Nick's dark eyes. She wished she didn't blush so easily because she felt the effects burned into her cheeks as Nick stared at her and Darcy who would never let it go that she was having coffee with a man. Just because Darcy was deliriously happy now that she was married to Joshua didn't mean everyone else had to be. Where her best friend got that idea was beyond Jesse—well, maybe she did know since she usually felt that way, except for herself.

Darcy stopped at the table. "Jesse, I'm so glad to see you today. I had a brainstorm last night and was going to call you after I talked with Beth about it. I—"

Darcy's voice faded into the silence. Jesse tore her gaze from Nick's and looked at her friend who swung her attention from Jesse to Nick then back. "Have I interrupted something?"

Jesse saw the gleam sparkle in Darcy's eyes and immediately said, "No, we were just waiting for Cindy, Nate, Boswell and Gramps to show up."

"I know who Nate and Gramps are. Who are Cindy and Boswell?"

"Cindy is my daughter and Boswell works for me." Nick held out his hand. "I'm Nick Blackburn, Jesse's neighbor."

"Oh," Darcy said, drawing that one simple word out and putting more meaning into it than she normally would. "I'm Darcy Markham. I've known Jesse for years. We went to school together."

While Nick wrapped his hand around Darcy's and shook it, Jesse asked, "What did you want to tell me?" hoping that would take her friend's mind off what was obviously dancing about inside Darcy's head. Jesse had been a matchmaker too long not to see the signs in another, and she was not going to be a party to anyone trying to fix her up.

Darcy dragged her attention from Nick and regarded Jesse. "We can talk later. I wouldn't want to interrupt anything." She started to leave.

Jesse caught her arm and held her in place. "No way, Darcy Markham."

Her friend grinned. "Say that again."

"What? *No way?* Or *Darcy Markham?*"

"Darcy Markham." A dreamy look glazed Darcy's eyes. "Darcy just got married a few months ago—actually

Valentine's Day, so you have to forgive her getting side-tracked when you say her new name. Now, back to my original question, what did you need to tell me?"

"I thought we would form a group, maybe meet Saturday afternoons to talk."

"Who, you and me? We talk all the time."

"I thought maybe you, me, Beth, Zoey and Tanya. Zoey and I just moved back to Sweetwater and Tanya— well, she could use some—" Darcy glanced away then back "—some support. I'd better go. I'll talk with Beth about it and get back to you later. Nice to meet you, Mr. Blackburn." Darcy hurried toward Beth seated at a table near the door.

Jesse watched her friend for a few seconds longer. There was more to this group than Darcy was willing to say in front of Nick.

"I'm beginning to think you really *do* know everyone in Sweetwater." Nick's voice cut into her thoughts and pulled her attention away from Darcy and toward him. "Of course, I haven't met Zoey or Tanya yet, but I do think I met everyone else today while hanging up posters."

Jesse shifted in her seat in the booth. "We had to get the word out about Oreo. I wonder where everyone else is."

Nick stared out the large plate glass window that ran the length of the front of the café. "I see Nate, Cindy and your grandfather coming now. Do you think your grandfather is okay?"

Jesse spied the group on the sidewalk across the street.

Gramps leaned against the post waiting for the stoplight to turn green while the two children danced about him, barely containing their energy. "Gramps keeps telling me he's too mean to get sick. My son has him wrapped around his finger. He'd do anything for Nate."

"That must be nice."

The hard edge to Nick's voice piqued her interest. "Do you have any grandparents alive?"

He shrugged. "I don't know."

"You don't?" she said before she could stop the words.

"I left home—such as it was—when I was sixteen."

"You were a runaway?"

Nick picked up his glass, his hand clenched so tightly about it that Jesse wondered if he would break it. "You have to have a home in the first place to be able to run away from one."

"You were living on the streets?" Sweetwater was small enough that the people who lived there took care of anyone in need, so the concept was new to Jesse even though she had read about it happening in other places.

Nick's tensed expression eased as he looked beyond Jesse. He smiled. "How did it go, princess?"

Cindy slid into the booth next to her father. "Everyone said they would look for Oreo. We stopped at the church and said a prayer for him. Nate said it would help."

Nate sat next to Jesse. "Yeah, Mom always says a prayer can work miracles."

"Daddy, I hope God listened to me."

Nick put his arm about his daughter. "I'm sure He did."

Jesse didn't think Cindy heard the doubt in her father's voice, but she had. Nick's gaze caught hers and held it for a few seconds. There was more than doubt in Nick's eyes—there was a bleakness that ripped through Jesse's defenses. Cindy needed a mother, but Nick needed much more than that. He needed to believe in the power of the Lord. He needed to believe in life again. He might think their conversation was over because of the arrival of the children, but she had every intention of continuing it later.

"Are you sure about ordering pizza?" Nick asked as he came up behind Jesse on the deck of her house.

She surveyed the darkening sky to the west, a large bank of ominous-looking clouds rolling in. A surge of panic zipped up her spine, and she determinedly shoved it into the background. "Yes. Boswell deserves a night off after finding Oreo today." *And I don't want to be alone,* she added silently, the wind picking up, the temperature dropping rapidly.

"This is one father who is happy Boswell found Oreo by the lake. After going all over town today, I was sure the kitten was long gone or—"

"Or what?"

"Some animal's dinner." He looked toward the water.

"If you mean Fred and Ethel, they wouldn't do that."

He shook his head. "I was thinking about the owl I hear every morning when I drink my coffee on the deck. I've heard owls prey sometimes on animals like skunks. You have to admit Oreo could be mistaken for one."

"I hadn't thought of that." Jesse shivered, hugging her

arms to her, more from the cooling breeze than from what he had said.

"I may be a city guy, but I do know a few things about the country. One I just learned recently. Not to go near geese."

Jesse laughed, focusing on the man near her rather than the storm brewing. "I'm so glad you're a quick learner. Now if you would only rub off on Gramps."

"I heard him leaving not long after Boswell arrived."

"Probably for the best. He said he was going to Susan Reed's for dinner, but frankly I think he feels threatened by Boswell."

Nick's chuckle spiced the air. "Boswell can have that effect on a person. When he first came to work for me, I wasn't sure if we would last a week. But he was wonderful with Cindy and that counted a lot in my book. I must admit now that I don't think I could make it without him."

The dark cloud completely obliterated what light there had been from the setting sun. The only illumination on the deck came from the kitchen and den. Jesse felt the need to go inside, but she didn't want to break the mood by suggesting a change. She suspected that Nick didn't open up much about himself.

Instead, she leaned back against the railing, gripping its wood, and asked, "How long has Boswell worked for you?"

"Over three years."

"What made you hire a manservant? Isn't that a bit unusual?"

"Actually I had advertised for a nanny-housekeeper."

"And Boswell applied?"

"Sort of. A friend suggested him and after meeting him I decided he was the best person qualified for the job. I always hire the best."

"What did your wife have to say about it?" The second she had spoken the question Jesse wished she could have taken it back. A cloud as dark as the one in the sky dropped over his features and the temperature seemed to fall even more.

"Brenda didn't care."

There was a wealth of unspoken emotions in those simple words that struck a chord with Jesse. His pain wrapped about her heart and squeezed. She reached out to touch his arm and he took a step back. The rejection hurt.

"I'm sorry."

"What's there to be sorry about? My wife didn't want to be involved with the mundane household chores like cleaning, shopping, cooking. That's why I hired Boswell."

So much more wasn't being said, Jesse realized as she watched Nick shut down his emotions, not one shred of evidence of what he was feeling visible on his expression. She needed to watch what she said. She was way too curious for her own good. It was obvious he didn't want to talk about the past and all the prodding on her part wasn't going to change that.

She shoved herself away from the railing, noticing a piece of paper swirling on the wind and racing across the deck. She snatched it from the crevice it was lodged in and balled it into her fist. "I'd better order that pizza now. I don't know about you, but I'm starved."

Silence greeted her announcement and heightened her unease.

She entered the kitchen while Nick stayed out on the deck. After calling in the order, she started for the back door and stopped herself. He needed time alone or he would have come inside when she had. She always wanted to fix everyone's problems when some people didn't want her to. She needed to learn to back off when the message was loud and clear.

Jesse began setting out the plates and napkins for the pizza. The back door opened and closed. The atmosphere in the kitchen sharpened as though someone was taking a knife and honing it to a razor's edge.

"I'm sorry if I opened old wounds. I didn't mean to," Jesse said, not facing Nick as she shut the cabinet. She didn't want to see no emotions on his face; she didn't want to see that bleak look, either. Both bothered her.

The sound of his footsteps cut through the silence that hung in the air. She felt him near, could smell his particular lime-scented aftershave. She licked her dry lips, pushed herself off from the counter and whirled around to face him. He was only a foot away, so close she could touch the hard planes of his face, smooth his frown away—if she chose to. She kept her arms at her sides as though frozen. In that moment she felt as though she would shatter into a thousand icy particles.

"No, I'm the one who is sorry. I'm not used to having…a friend. You were only trying to find out about me."

The word *friend* came out stiff sounding, as though he had never said it before. If truth be told, she wasn't used to having a male friend. She had many females as friends but not a man. She forced a smile to her mouth. "Yes, friend. I figured you needed someone to show you around Sweetwater. After all, you're going to be here for two months."

"And you've decided you're that person?"

"We're neighbors. That's what neighbors do for each other."

"Not in Chicago."

"Well, in Sweetwater they do and since you're in Sweetwater, you're stuck with me." Again the second she had said the sentence, she wanted to take it back. What was it about this evening that was making her say things she shouldn't? Must be the storm brewing. She hated bad weather. She acted irrationally with no fore-thought to what she was going to say.

One corner of his mouth lifted. "You make it sound like a sentence."

"You might feel that way before it's over," she said in a flippant tone, wanting to lighten the mood before she began to confess all her deep, dark secrets—or worse, he did. Then she would have to do something about them.

"Can I help you with anything? Set the table? Wash your windows?"

"If I thought you were serious about the window washing, I'd take you up on the offer another day. Haven't you noticed there's a storm brewing?"

"Kinda hard to miss. It was spitting rain when I came in."

"Then just in case we'd better get a few flashlights out."

"Does the electricity go off a lot when it storms here?"

"No, but I like to be prepared." Then she might feel she had some control over the bad weather. "How is Cindy when it storms?"

He thought a moment. "She's usually okay. Our apartment is well insulated. It has to be a really bad storm for us to hear it."

"I wish I could say that. This house is old and I think we can hear a pin drop outside."

"How is Nate?"

"Fine. He's like his father. He loved a good thunderstorm." *Better than me,* she wanted to add, but hoped no one discovered her weakness. She tried to put up a brave front for the family, but it was getting more difficult. She had never done well in a storm before Mark was struck by lightning. Now she came apart inside with each sound of thunder and flash of lightning. On one level she knew her actions were way out of proportion to what was going on, but on a deeper level it didn't make any difference.

"Where are your flashlights?"

"I have several in the drawer by the refrigerator and a couple in the drawer in the coffee table in the den."

"You *are* prepared." Nick retrieved the two flashlights from the kitchen drawer, then headed toward the den.

While he was gone, Jesse stared out the window over the sink, listening to the wind brush the limbs of the oak tree against the house and the raindrops pelt the panes as though they were fingernails trying to claw their way inside. Her hands clutched the counter so hard they ached. It had begun and from the looks of the clouds earlier it would be a doozy. She shouldn't have invited Nick, Cindy and Boswell to dinner—to watch her fall apart. If she hadn't, she could have closeted herself in her bedroom and huddled under the covers until it was over.

"I've got two more flashlights. Anything else you want me to do?"

Jesse caught herself before she gasped. She hadn't heard him returning, so lost in thoughts of the storm. *Focus on the man,* she told herself and turned toward Nick. "No, I think all we need now are the pizzas and we'll be set."

Not a minute later the doorbell chimed. "Want me to get it while you get Boswell and the children?" Nick asked, already walking toward the front door.

Jesse spotted her money on the counter and started to go after Nick. She stopped herself, realizing he had intentionally ignored it because he had decided he would pay for the pizzas, had stated that very thing when she had suggested ordering out. In that second she realized Nick Blackburn was a force to be reckoned with—like the storm.

She made her way to Nate's room and found Cindy and her son on the floor playing with Bingo and Oreo. Boswell sat on Nate's bed watching the two children, not one expression crossing his face—not even boredom. She could see where Nick would think that Boswell was perfect for him. They both didn't show much of what they were thinking. *Two of a kind,* she thought with a laugh.

"The pizzas are here. Wash up and come to the kitchen."

Nate hopped up. "You ordered pepperoni, didn't you?"

"Of course."

"Yes!" He pumped his arm in the air. "Mama Mia makes the best pepperoni pizza." He raced past Jesse with Cindy following on his heels.

Boswell pushed himself off the bed. "If what young Master Nate has been telling us is true, then we are in for a delightful treat."

"If you like pizza, then, yes, you are. You can't beat Mama Mia's."

"Is she Italian?" Boswell motioned for her to leave before him.

"Mama Mia is a man named Charlie and about as American as apple pie and baseball."

"I see."

"You do? I'm not sure I do. I went to school with Charlie and all of us knew any restaurant he opened would be successful. He was a great cook as a teenager. He just thought the name Mama Mia would help him when he first opened his restaurant ten years ago. We tried to tell Charlie *his* name would go further than a made-up one."

"Some people don't believe enough in themselves and put on a facade for others."

Jesse glanced at Boswell and wondered whom he

was talking about. Himself? Nick? Someone else? Was the man lonely? Did he have a girlfriend in Chicago? Maybe she should try to fix him up as well as his employer. "Well, Charlie has plenty of confidence now. He's opened a chain of these pizza parlors all over Kentucky. Quite successful but still lives here and is very involved in the original restaurant. We're lucky in Sweetwater."

When Jesse entered the kitchen, the children had finished washing their hands and were drying them with paper towels. Nick had placed the boxes of pizzas on the table and the aroma peppered the air with smells of cheese, bread, meat and spices. Jesse's mouth watered. Fear always made her hungry.

As she sat at the table, the first rumble of thunder followed by a flash of lightning made her stiffen, gripping the edge of her chair. She glanced around, hoping no one noticed the fear she imagined etched into her features about now. Again she wondered why she had invited her neighbors to witness her falling apart. She generally avoided even Darcy and Beth who knew so many of her secrets while growing up.

Nate started to reach for a piece of pizza. Jesse gave him a stern look. He snatched his hand back and bowed his head. Cindy followed suit while Nick frowned and Boswell stared.

"Remember we say a prayer before eating," Jesse said and folded her hands in front of her. "Dear Heavenly Father, bless this food that we are about to enjoy. Watch over those less fortunate then us and provide us with the means to help them when we can. Amen." Silently she added, *And help me to get through this evening without making a fool of myself.*

When she brought her head up, she found Nick lifting his and she was relieved that he had gone along with the prayer. She got the impression that he hadn't stepped foot in a church in a long time, if ever. Maybe that was why they had moved next door for the summer. Maybe she was supposed to show him the power of the Lord in a person's life. Nick was hurting deep inside. She wanted to help. And in the process maybe help Cindy find a mother.

"Isn't this great?" her son said while his mouth was stuffed with pepperoni pizza.

"Nate! Please wait until you finish eating your food before you talk."

Her son gulped down a mouthful of food, then washed it down with some milk. "Sorry." He turned to Cindy who was next to him. "What do ya think?"

The young girl bit off a more delicate bite than her son and chewed it thoroughly before answering, "Great! You were right."

Nate puffed out his chest. "Of course. I know the best places in town for food."

"My son, the connoisseur."

"What's that?" Nate took another big bite of his pizza.

"An expert, in this case of food." Boswell used his fork to cut off some of his slice and brought it to his mouth.

"Yep, that's me. I know the best place to get a fudge sundae, a hamburger, fries. You name it. I can tell you where to go."

Another crack of thunder sounded with lightning striking close by. Jesse jumped, nearly choking on her food. She began to cough. Nick patted her back while tears filled her eyes. A long moment later she breathed normally again and took a large swallow of her water.

"Mom, you okay?"

She waved her hand. "Just went down the wrong way."

"Mom doesn't like storms," her traitorous son announced to the whole table.

Everyone regarded her. She could feel the heat burning her cheeks. "I—I—" What could she say to that?

"When it storms really bad, she usually hides out in her room."

"Nate, I don't think my habits need to be discussed at the table." Jesse clenched her hands in her lap and pinched her lips together.

"Sorry, Mom. I just wanted them to know why you jumped."

Her jaw ached from gritting her teeth. Her nails dug into her palms. When more thunder rumbled the walls and lightning scorched a path through the air not far from the window, Jesse managed only to flinch, but her fists tightened even more. She nearly came unglued when she felt Nick's hand cover hers. She slanted a look at him and saw him wink. Something inside her relaxed a bit even though the wind and rain slashed at the house.

"I saw, Master Nate, that you had the game Trouble. Anyone up for a rousing game of Trouble?"

"I am," Cindy said, leaping to her feet with a piece of pizza in her hand.

"Me, too." Nate stood, finishing his last bite. "Can we take our food to the den and play a game, Mom?"

"Fine."

"I'll make sure they don't get any food on the furniture." Boswell scooted his chair back and rose, while the children grabbed up a piece of pizza and raced from the room.

"I will supervise the children while you finish eating."

When Boswell left, the silence lasted for a few seconds then thunder filled it, reminding her that a storm raged outside—not that she had ever forgotten except for a few seconds when Nick had touched her hands and winked at her. "We'd better clean up this mess."

"That's something I can handle."

Jesse began taking the plates over to the sink. "I don't get the impression you do too many dishes."

"I have in the past."

"You did?"

"Distant past. When I was working my way through college, I had a variety of jobs. One was being a dishwasher at a fancy restaurant. I took pride in the fact that I didn't break one piece of china or crystal."

"I am impressed. How long did you wash dishes?"

"Two days."

Jesse laughed. "What happened?"

"I convinced the owner I would be better suited as a busboy."

"How long did that last?"

"Three days. I became a waiter at the restaurant when one didn't show up and stayed for two years. The pay wasn't great, but the tips were. Funded my last two years of college."

"So you're the kind of guy who seizes the moment."

"Definitely." Nick opened the dishwasher and took the first plate that Jesse rinsed off. "That job taught me a few lessons."

"What?"

"Hard work pays off. And how to grit my teeth when someone was being condescending. That it's better to be rich than poor. After working there, I decided I wanted to be one of the people who was waited *on*, not the waiter."

"There's more than one way to be rich in life than having money."

"When you grow up poor, scrambling for something decent to eat, it doesn't seem that way. I have a feeling we came from two very different backgrounds. You grew up here in Sweetwater, right?"

"Yes."

"You probably never wanted for a thing."

She turned so she could face him, not one expression visible on his features. "I had a good childhood. My father made a nice income. My mother didn't work outside the home. We went to church every week. I was a cheerleader, class secretary in high school and on the girl's softball team. A pretty normal childhood for Sweetwater."

"But not for me on the streets of Chicago. My father left my mom when I was two so I never really knew my father's family. Mom worked two jobs to try to put some food on the table and keep a roof over our heads. Sometimes she was successful, other times not. I can remember days going without much food except peanut butter sandwiches. We didn't even have money for the jelly. To this day I can't eat peanut butter."

She reached toward him. "I'm sorry."

He took a step back, staring at her outstretched hand. "What for? It wasn't your fault." He pivoted toward the table and strode to it to pick up the last of the dirty dishes.

His stiff back drew her toward him. She started to move forward but stopped herself. She knew by his earlier actions that he would reject any offer of comfort. Swinging back toward the sink, she grabbed a glass.

Thunder and lightning, close and deafening, shook the house.

Taken off guard, she jerked back and the glass slipped from her nerveless fingers. In slow motion she watched it crash to the floor, shattering into hundreds of shards at her feet.

Another round of thunder and lightning sent her back against a solid wall of human flesh. Arms held her and turned her around. The comfort she had wanted to offer Nick was evident in the softened expression on his face. His arms wound about her and drew her to him.

For a few seconds she forgot the storm. She felt as though she'd come home.

Chapter Five

The jasmine scent that he'd come to associate with Jesse inundated Nick. For a few seconds it felt so right to hold this woman to him and give her the comfort she needed. Then his memories flooded him like her scent, and he realized the danger in getting too close to Jesse Bradshaw. She could make him wish he were different, that he had never known the heartache of being married to Brenda.

From an early age he had learned to be a survivor and the only way he knew to survive was to distance himself from anything or anyone who might hurt him. He hadn't with Brenda and he had paid dearly for that mistake. The dull pain in his leg when he did too much was a reminder if he ever dared to forget.

He continued to hold Jesse who trembled in his arms. The warmth from her body threatened to melt his defenses. He fought to keep them intact, desperation vying with his needs as a man that he'd kept buried for over a year.

Finally he stepped back, his hands clasping her upper arms. "Are you all right?" He heard the slight quaver to his words and winced at the vulnerability he was exhibiting. Never show your weakness to another, he had been taught through the years when he had struggled to take care of himself after his mother's death. And Brenda certainly had reinforced that when their marriage had begun to fall apart.

Jesse's green eyes glistened with unshed tears. "No—yes." She shook her head. "I don't know. Nate was right about me not handling storms very well."

"We all have things we are afraid of."

"What is yours?"

Being asked that question, he wanted to say. Instead, he shrugged and decided to tell her the partial truth. "Going hungry." He'd told Jesse more of his past than he had anyone else except Brenda. And in the end his deceased wife had used that knowledge to hurt him. He couldn't believe he had disclosed so much to Jesse. He hadn't known her long, and yet she was so easy to talk to—to make him want to forget his past. That realization sent panic through him. He hardened his heart, determined not to give in to the weakness of wanting to be needed.

"Thankfully that's not likely going to happen to you."

"Whereas storms will always be around?"

"Yes." She shoved her hand through her short brown hair. "I never liked thunderstorms as a child, but when I lost Mark to a lightning strike, my fear multiplied. I'm the reason—" She bit her bottom lip to keep it from trembling. A tear leaked from her eye and ran down her cheek. Turning away, she swiped at her face. "I can finish cleaning up later."

"I can stay as long as you need me." The only person who had really needed him was Cindy, and he felt as if he had let her down on more than one occasion.

"You don't have to baby-sit me. I've lived with this irrational fear for over thirty years. I'll manage."

The quavering in her voice belied her tough words. He clasped her shoulder. "Why don't we join Cindy and Nate and play a game of Trouble?"

Looking back at him, she smiled but the edges of her mouth quivered. "You just want to take advantage of my weakened resolve."

"You've discovered my strategy."

"I must warn you I am very competitive—" she cocked her head and listened "—and I think the storm is moving away from here."

"What a nice challenge. You at your peak."

Her laughter saturated the air, all traces of the tension of the past hour gone. "I could say the same thing about you."

He swept his arm across his body and indicated the door that led to the den. "I thrive on a good challenge."

"Let me pick up the broken glass first, then I'll gladly thrash you at a game of Trouble." She bent down to begin the task.

"I'll help." He knelt next to her, his arm brushing against hers.

The casual touch was like a bolt of lightning streaking up his arm. He felt the electricity zip through his body and nearly dropped the piece of glass he had picked up. He steadied himself, drawing in a deep, composing breath. His senses were imbued with her scent of jasmine, and he was right back where he was a few minutes ago—needing and wanting something that would be no good for him.

When the glass was cleaned up, he put several feet between them. "On second thought, I'd better call it an evening. I forgot I still have some calls to make overseas. Now that the storm is abating we should be able to get home without getting too drenched."

Disappointment fretted across her features. "I can loan you a couple of umbrellas. You can bring them back tomorrow."

"Sure. I'd better go get Cindy and Boswell." He backed away, his gaze caught in hers. He felt like a coward, tossing down a challenge then reneging. That wasn't his usual method of operation. But he was a survivor and he needed his space before he did something foolish. Jesse Bradshaw was the marrying kind, and he would never marry again because he was a survivor.

Nick leaned close to Jesse and whispered, "I can't believe you talked me into this class."

"Don't tell me you're one of those people who doesn't like to get his hands dirty."

"I think we're past that."

Spying Nick's hands covered with paste used in making his papier-mâché animal, Jesse laughed. "I think you're right. What is that, by the way?"

"I'm crushed. You can't tell it's a cat?"

She tried to contain her laughter but wasn't very successful. "Sorry. Where's its tail?"

"It's a tailless cat." He looked offended, but merriment frolicked in his eyes. He nodded toward her papier-mâché animal. "What's that?"

"A dog and this is his tail." Jesse pointed to a stub at one end of a blob of paper pulp.

"If you say so."

"Daddy, what do you think?"

"Sweetie, you've done a great job with your, er—" he studied his daughter's art project "—rabbit."

"It's not a rabbit. I decided to do a bird." Cindy slapped on some more wet paper.

"Oh, great bird. Now that I look at it closer I can see its wings." He pointed toward the area sticking out of the side.

"That's his beak and that's his tail."

"Yes. Yes. Tail and beak."

Jesse pressed her lips together, but her laughter continued to bubble up inside her. She bent toward Nick and whispered, "You need to learn to let your child tell you first what they did before committing yourself."

"Committing myself is the optimum phrase here. I'm definitely not projecting an image of an industry leader."

"No, but you are projecting an image of a wonderful, devoted father."

"I am? Well, in that case, it's all worth it." He studied Cindy's papier-mâché animal, his brow wrinkled in a thoughtful look. "She told me earlier she was doing a rabbit."

"Sometimes they change their minds. Be vague and let them talk about their artwork."

"Mom, I'm finished. Do you like it?"

"Nate, I love your animal. What a neat choice of colors."

"I know horses aren't blue, but it's my favorite color."

After properly admiring her son's work, she mouthed the word, "see," to Nick. He inclined his head.

Beth Coleman stood at the front of the room. "Class, when you're through making your animals, we're going to let them dry and you can take them home next Saturday. If you haven't finished painting your project, we'll have some time next week to complete it. It's time to clean up."

"Painting! I haven't finished making my animal." Nick picked up his project and one of the legs fell off. "This is why I didn't put a tail on my cat. I'm having a hard enough time with the four legs."

"Daddy, your cat looks funny."

"You think?"

Cindy giggled. "I'll help you next week."

"I think I'm a lost cause." He took his three-legged cat to the shelf to store it.

Jesse hung back, letting him talk to Beth who was supervising the storing of the projects. They spoke a brief moment—not nearly long enough to make a proper connection—then he headed back to the table.

As Cindy and Nate left to put their projects on the shelf, Jesse said, "Don't you think Beth is wonderful with the children?"

Nick stopped cleaning up the mess he'd made and looked at Jesse. "Sure."

"She has the patience of Job."

"I'm sure she does."

"I'm surprised she isn't married with a horde of children of her own. She would make a great mother."

Nick's eyes narrowed. "Why are you telling me this?"

"I don't want you to worry about Cindy if you can't come. She'll be in good hands."

"You mean I don't have to come and do the art projects each week?"

This conversation wasn't going the way she wanted, Jesse thought. In fact, the whole class hadn't gone as she had wanted. Beth had hardly paid much attention to Nick. Of course, with Jimmy throwing up at the beginning of class then Cal trying to eat the paste she hadn't had much time to pay attention to anyone. "Beth encourages the parents to participate, but you don't have to."

"That's a relief." He wiped his hand across his forehead before he realized it was still covered with partially wet papier-mâché paste.

Jesse knew the second he remembered his hands weren't clean. His eyes widened as he rolled them skyward as though he could see the white trail he'd left on his forehead.

"I'm definitely more comfortable in a boardroom than a classroom." He snatched up a paper towel and cleaned his forehead. Then he looked down at his jeans and T-shirt and grimaced. "Boswell won't be too happy with me. I think I have more paste on my clothes than the project."

"Believe me, it washes out."

"I suppose with kids it would have to."

"Definitely." Jesse saw Beth hurrying by and said, "Beth, can I help with anything?"

Her friend stopped, took a deep breath and pushed her hair back behind her ear. "Class usually isn't this hectic."

"You remember Nick Blackburn from the other day at the café."

Beth started to offer her hand, then remembered it was covered with paint and just smiled instead. "Yes. You have an adorable little girl."

"Yes, isn't Cindy cute?" Jesse shifted to allow another parent by, which caused Nick to have to move closer to Beth. Things were looking up. Maybe she would be able to stop searching for someone for Nick.

"Thank you. I think she'll enjoy this class, but I may not always be able to come. Will it be okay if someone else brings her?"

"Sure, whatever works best for you. The important thing is that Cindy enjoys herself. I've got to go and catch Cal's mother before she leaves. I'm glad Cindy will be joining the class."

As soon as Beth left, Nick busied himself cleaning up his work area, then washing his hands, his glance not once straying toward Beth. Disappointment sagged

Jesse's shoulders as she stood back and tried to decide
what had gone wrong. Why couldn't she find someone
for Nick? Beth would be perfect. Why couldn't either
one of them see that?

Another plan popped into her mind as the members
of the class began to leave. Slowly Jesse straightened
her area, cleaned the table off and washed her hands,
too. Cindy and Nate danced about, trying to contain
their energy but not doing a very good job. Even Nick
finished and watched Jesse with a furrowed brow.

"Do you need help?" he asked, picking up her art
project to take over to the shelf.

There was only one more student in the class. Jesse
purposefully moved in slow motion as she gathered up
her purse. Beth said goodbye to Cheryl and her mother.

Jesse checked her watch. "It's nearly lunchtime. Why
don't we get something to eat at the hamburger joint
across the street?"

As she knew they would, both Cindy and Nate
said, "Yes!"

"How can I say no?"

"You can't. Let's see if Beth would like to join us."
Before Nick could reply, Jesse rushed toward her friend.
"We're going to get some hamburgers at Joe's Diner.
Want to come?"

"Sorry, Jesse. I've got to meet with Reverend Collins
about the Fourth of July auction before I meet you at
Darcy's. Some other time."

Beth grabbed her purse and headed toward the door
to the classroom before Jesse could form a reply. *Lord,*

are You telling me to pass on this one? Nothing seems to work with Nick. I need some help here. I'm not doing a very good job with this man.

"Our teacher has other plans?"

Nick's deep husky voice sent a shiver down her spine. She wheeled around. "Yes." Her voice came out breathless as though she had run in a marathon. Her chest barely seemed able to contain the beating of her heart.

"Then can we leave now?"

"Sure."

With Nate and Cindy leading the way, Jesse and Nick walked from the school building and across the street to Joe's Diner. The aromas of grilled meat and French fries drew Jesse like a magnet. She loved all the wrong foods for a woman who should watch her weight.

Nick paused at the door. "Do you think I look okay to eat out in public?" He gestured toward his less than clean clothes.

"No better than I." Jesse waved her hand down the length of her attire of knee-length blue shorts and white T-shirt with splashes of paste and paint. "I don't think Joe will mind." Glancing through the picture window, Jesse added, "Besides, I see several other class participants inside so we won't be the only ones."

"Thank goodness none of my acquaintances in Chicago can see me now. They would be shocked."

"Because of your clothes or because of the place you are eating lunch at?" Jesse entered the diner in front of Nick and weaved her way toward the table in the back where the children had already camped out. Joe's Diner had simple fare and was plainly decorated with wooden tables and chairs that had seen many years of customers, and few objects adorning the white walls.

"Both. I actually had to go buy some more casual clothes after being here for several days and realizing my wardrobe wasn't small-town America."

"I suppose three-piece suits are a little out of place in Sweetwater. Mind you, we do occasionally wear our good clothes but mostly overalls and jeans are the mainstay of our wardrobe," Jesse said with a straight face.

Nick stared at her for a long moment, then chuckled. "I deserved that. And for the record, I don't wear three-piece suits. Too stuffy for me." He slid a chair out for Jesse and waited until she sat before he took the seat next to her.

"Daddy, can I order anything I want?" Cindy opened the menu and tilted her head to the side as though she was enthralled with what was written on the paper before her.

"Maybe."

Peering around the side of her menu, Cindy screwed up her face into a frown. "Maybe?"

"I'm not saying yes until I hear what it is you want. The last time I said yes without knowing the terms I was stuck with a set of books you haven't even looked at since you got them."

"What are you having, Nate?" Cindy asked, going back to studying her menu.

"The hamburgers are the best in town and you can't beat Joe's French fries. But I also like the onion rings, too."

"I want all that, Daddy."

"French fries *and* onion rings?" One of Nick's eyebrows rose.

Cindy nodded. "And a hamburger with chocolate milk."

"That's an awful lot to eat."

Cindy closed her menu and straightened in her chair. "I'm mighty hungry after all that work this morning."

Nate slapped his menu down. "I'll have the same, too."

"Are you gonna eat it this time? The last time you didn't finish half your burger." Jesse collected the menus and waved to Lila to let her know they were ready to order.

"I'm hungry, too. Gramps says I'm a growing boy who needs fuel to grow."

"That's an interesting way to put it," Nick said, unwrapping his silverware and placing his paper napkin in his lap.

"So you're gonna eat every bit of it this time?"

Nate bobbed his head up and down.

When Lila came to take their orders, Nick told her what they wanted—hamburgers and French fries for everyone with two extra side dishes of onion rings.

After she left, Jesse took a drink of her water. "I hope Dr. Wilson doesn't see us eating this. This goes against every diet I've heard of."

"Don't tell me you watch your weight?" Nick said with a laugh.

"Yes. If I don't, who will?"

His gaze roamed down the length of her. "I can think of a few who might."

Heat flamed her cheeks at the amused look—with a

hint of something she didn't dare put a name to—in his eyes. She needed to champion Beth before she forgot her mission to find Nick a suitable wife. "What did you think of the art class today?"

"Do I have to go back?"

"Daddy, I want to go next Saturday."

Nick turned his attention to his daughter. "*You* can, princess. It's me we're talking about."

"You don't wanna go?" Cindy squirmed in her chair, a pout forming.

"Yes, Nick, you don't want to go?"

Nick threw Jesse a narrowed look before addressing his daughter. "I'm not very good at creating art."

"Daddy, you don't have to be." She dropped her head and stared at the table.

"Cindy, if you want to go, I'll take you, but I'm not promising you that I'll participate."

"That's okay, Daddy. Jesse will be there to help me if I need it. Maybe she can help you."

"Sure, Nick. I'd be glad to." Jesse contained her laughter that threatened. Nick probably wouldn't appreciate it. She doubted he was put in the hot seat much, and the man definitely looked as though he wanted to squirm in his chair.

"I think I can manage but thanks for the offer," Nick said, relief on his face as the waitress placed the plates of food in front of everyone, effectively ending the conversation.

Jesse leaned toward Nick and whispered, "Beth is a wonderful teacher. Cindy and *you* will learn a lot."

"I'm sure Beth is, but papier-mâché isn't my idea of art."

"Beauty is in the eye of the beholder."

Nick took a bite of his hamburger. "Mmm. This is delicious."

Jesse noted the surprise in his voice and couldn't help responding, "There's nothing fancy about Joe's food, but it is great tasting."

"I can appreciate a hamburger with the best of them." Nick bit down again and chewed slowly as though savoring it.

"Daddy, can I go to church with Nate tomorrow?"

Lifting his hamburger toward his mouth, Nick stopped in mid motion. He peered at Jesse.

"It's okay with me. I would love for Cindy to come with us. You can, too, if you want."

Nick shifted in his chair, putting his hamburger down on his plate. "Sweetie, if you want to go that's fine with me."

"Will you come?" Cindy picked up her milk and took a long drink.

"I can't, princess."

"Why can't you come?"

"I have some business that I need to take care of."

Cindy cocked her head and stared at him. "On Sunday?"

"Some overseas calls. Maybe some other time." Nick shifted again in his chair.

Jesse wondered about the uncomfortable expression on Nick's face. Did he believe in God? He was allowing Cindy to go to church and yet he wouldn't go himself. She had the feeling there was more to the story than overseas calls.

"Don't forget later on this afternoon Boswell said we could finish that Trouble game we started the other night. I'll bring it over to your house." Nate wiped his mouth then wadded his paper napkin and put it by his empty plate.

"Ah, I seem to remember a challenge about a game. But then someone had to leave before making good on his challenge." Jesse popped an onion ring into her mouth, relishing the taste of the batter that Joe used.

"I'll play you a game of Trouble any place, any time," Nick said, tossing down his napkin in a dramatic display.

Jesse's gaze locked onto Nick's. "Fine. I'll come over after I go to Darcy's this afternoon." Beth always went to church and this would be a great opportunity to throw them together again. And just maybe Nick would see the power of the Lord at work. Maybe while playing a game of Trouble she could find a way to persuade Nick to accompany his daughter to church.

"You're on," he said, his gaze boring into her with an intensity that rocked her.

When Jesse glanced away, she caught her son and Cindy staring at them. For a few minutes she had forgotten the children were sitting at the table with them. And she suspected Nick had, too, if his ashened features were any indication when he looked toward Nate and Cindy.

"Every time I see this beautiful bookcase, I want one in my house. If Joshua ever decides to start a side business on his days off, I'll be the first to order a built-in bookcase." Jesse stood in front of the beautifully carved piece of furniture being discussed, running her hand along its oak surface.

"What days off? If he's not investigating a fire, my dad has him at the farm, learning the business right alongside me." Darcy went to answer the doorbell that rang.

"How do you feel about that?"

As her friend put her hand on the knob, she said, "I'm fine with it. Dad and I have come to terms with me feeling as if he only wanted a son. I want both Sean and Joshua to learn the business. Joshua and I plan on having a large family. I'll need the backup." She opened the door and greeted Beth and Tanya.

As the ladies came into the living room and sat, Jesse asked, "Any news, Darcy?"

"I'm not pregnant…yet." She smiled. "But it's fun trying."

Beth blushed. Tanya laughed. And Jesse remembered.

"Does anyone want anything to drink while we wait for Zoey to arrive?"

Tanya and Beth shook their heads while Jesse said, "No."

"Wasn't she always late for everything?" Beth asked, smoothing her long jean skirt.

"You know, I think you're right. I'm glad she's come back home from Dallas but not under the circumstances." Darcy sat in one of the chairs with matching ottoman.

"It must be awful not knowing if your husband is dead or alive." Jesse took the other chair.

"I think the government has given up searching and has declared him dead." Beth put her sensible beige purse on the floor next to the couch.

"But still she will always wonder," Jesse murmured, realizing she didn't have to wonder about that at least. Finding her husband outside in the backyard after the horrendous sound of the lightning strike was still permanently etched into her mind. For a year she'd had nightmares reliving that.

"I went to see Tom a few days ago in prison." A frown marred Tanya's beautiful dark features. She clasped her hand to her mouth. "Oh, I'm sorry, Darcy. I shouldn't talk about him with you."

"It's okay, Tanya. I've forgiven Tom long ago. Pain can drive a person to do a lot of bad things."

That was one of the things she loved about Darcy, Jesse thought. Her friend had such a generous heart. Tom had almost accidentally killed Darcy when he had set fire to the barn she was in, and yet she could forgive the man. Darcy had embraced the true meaning of forgiveness when she had turned back to the Lord.

"We didn't talk long. He didn't have much to say. He looked thinner and pale. I can't help him."

"Who drove you to see him?" Jesse asked, remembering why Darcy had wanted to start this weekly group: to help Tanya who suffered from a manic depressive disorder and whose husband was in prison for arson. Jesse had to agree that Tanya needed a circle of friends and with Zoey's return home she suspected she did, too.

"Reverend Collins. He's been so good to me. I don't want him to retire at the end of this year."

Beth leaned forward. "I've tried to talk him out of it. In fact, I tried just this afternoon, but he feels it is his time."

"How did your meeting go with the reverend? I wish you could have come to lunch with us."

"My meeting with the reverend was fine. What I want to know, Jesse Bradshaw, is why are you constantly trying to throw me and Nick Blackburn together? Are you trying to matchmake?"

The silence in the house was deafening as everyone waited for Jesse to answer. She cleared her throat, aware all eyes were on her. "I simply asked you to lunch. Can't a friend do that without having an ulterior motive?"

"You're evading my question which means you are matchmaking. Jesse, I am *not* looking for a husband. After my youngest brother leaves for college next year, I'm traveling and seeing some of this world. I won't have time to be married then." Beth pinned her with her sharp gaze. "Nick seems like a nice man. Why don't you fix *yourself* up with him?"

Now it was Jesse's turn to squirm under the scrutiny of her friends. "Because I'm not looking for a husband, either. I had one."

"I'm too old and set in my ways to have one now."

Darcy chuckled. "Too old! Beth, you're only a few years older than us."

"But all of you have been married. I haven't ever."

"You can't put an age on marriage," Jesse said, rising, needing to move about.

Beth stood, too. "Right. You can't. So why aren't you looking for a husband? You were happily married for a long time. Why don't you want that again?"

The doorbell chiming drew everyone's attention toward Zoey's arrival. Jesse hung back, fighting the pressure building in her chest as though a band were around it, squeezing tight. In her mind's eye she could see Mark on the ground not moving, not breathing. When he had died, he had taken a part of her with him. She couldn't ever risk losing any more of herself. If so, there would be nothing left.

Chapter Six

Jesse started to ring Nick's doorbell, but stopped before pressing it. She turned away, the question Beth had asked her still plaguing her.

What is it about your new neighbor that threatens your peace of mind? Frankly, after seeing you two together, I think you're scared of the feeling he generates in you. Is that why you're trying to match him up with every female in town?

She had denied Beth's observation and hadn't answered her friend. She didn't have an answer. And that did frighten her.

Why was she trying to find him a wife? Yes, Cindy wanted a mother. What girl her age didn't? But why had she taken the job on? She was sure a man like Nick was capable of finding his own wife—if he was looking for one, which he kept telling her he wasn't. Like her. She wasn't looking for a spouse, either. So she needed to quit trying to fix him up with any woman who was breathing and walking around. He wasn't a threat to her peace of mind because neither one of them wanted a partner. She was safe.

With that thought she wheeled about and rang the bell. She would help Cindy as much as possible while she was in Sweetwater. That was the least she could do for the young girl. And if she could be a friend to Nick, that was fine, too.

Nick opened the door. When he saw her, he smiled and something inside her melted. Her resolve?

"Come in and save me from those two children."

Save him? How about herself? She felt her resolve slipping and fought to shore it up. He did have the greatest smile with a dimple in the left cheek. It lit his face and shone deep in his eyes with creases at their corners. That was it. She'd always liked the way a person smiled. Her husband had had a great smile, too.

"You're the adult. What could those two darlings possibly be doing?"

"Cheating. Ganging up on me to make sure none of my game pieces ever sees the light of day."

"Not Nate and Cindy. You must be imagining things."

"It's two against one. That's not playing fair."

"But that's life and life isn't always fair."

"Humph. No wonder Boswell gladly gave up playing so he could fix dinner." Nick gestured toward the den at the back of the house. "I think it's your turn to be their victim."

Jesse led the way, glancing back over her shoulder at Nick. "I thought you and I had a game to play."

"How did your meeting go with the ladies?"

"It wasn't exactly a meeting. It's just a few friends getting together."

"I've met Darcy and Beth. Who else was there?" Nick asked as they entered the den.

"Zoey and Tanya. If you go to church with us tomorrow, you can meet them. I'll introduce you to them."

"I haven't agreed to go to church."

"You will."

"I will?" One brow arched.

"The Lord is on my side. I mean to get you to church."

For a few seconds there was a panicked look in his eyes before he veiled it. "Are you trying to save my soul?"

"I'm trying to show you that you aren't alone in this world."

"It won't work. I've been alone for most of my life," he whispered close to her ear.

His breath tickled her neck. His words froze her heart for a beat. "That can always change if you want."

"Maybe I like my life the way it is. I answer to no one and I control my own destiny."

She turned slightly to face him. "That's sad."

Surprise flickered into his gaze. He took a step back, stunned for a moment. He started to say something when Cindy and Nate spotted them by the door.

"Daddy, ready for another game?"

"Mom, you can play, too."

Nick fixed his gaze onto his daughter. "I think it's Jesse's turn to play you all."

"But you can play, Daddy. There are four colors so there's enough for everyone."

"I need to help Boswell with dinner. Do you want to join us for dinner, Jesse and Nate?"

Jesse started to say no when her son piped in, "Yeah, what are you having?"

"Tacos."

"Great. I love tacos."

"Boswell knows how to make tacos?" Jesse asked, having a hard time picturing Boswell preparing anything less than English or French cuisine.

"He's lived in this country for a long time. He's picked up a few American habits. He loves Mexican food."

Cindy hopped to her feet. "Nate and me can help him. He's let me before. You and Jesse have a game to play. Remember, Daddy?"

Nick grinned with none of the warmth of earlier. "How can I forget? Fine. We'll play our match while you two help Boswell."

Cindy and Nate raced from the room, leaving Jesse with Nick by the door. Trouble was set up on the game table in front of the picture window that looked out over Sweetwater Lake. Ducks and geese swam on its surface, smooth as glass. Peace reigned outside while inside trouble was brewing.

Nick swept his arm across his body. "After you. I'll even let you pick which color you want to be and go first."

Jesse sat at the table, toying with a yellow and a red piece. "I can't decide which of these colors I want. I like both of them."

"Yellow suits you more. You're always so upbeat." Nick took the blue pieces and put them in the game board.

"Is there a reason you picked blue?"

"It's my favorite color. I have no trouble picking what piece I will use."

"Decisive. Sure."

"Yep."

"I don't have a favorite color. The color I like will depend on my mood. Some days it is yellow. Others red or orange. Sometimes even green or blue."

"Indecisive? Unsure?"

"Nope. I don't like to lock myself down to only one favorite color. God made so many beautiful colors that I like them all. I don't like to limit myself. I like to keep myself open for all the possibilities life has to offer." Jesse selected the yellow pieces to use.

"How did we get into a philosophical discussion when all we were doing was picking our game pieces?"

She shrugged, tossing the die in her palm. "Just getting to know my neighbor."

"I can get impatient when things are going too slow. Throw the die."

"My, my. You are testy this evening." She rolled the die and it came up a three.

Snatching it up, he smiled, this time the deep, warm, toe-curling one. "Just thought I would speed your getting to know me along faster."

When the die came up four, he passed it to her. "That's so sweet, Nick, but what I love about getting to know someone new is delving into what makes the person tick."

"Did you make that last statement to rattle me?"

"Why, no. I would never resort to using tricks to win." She grinned, enjoying the dismay that appeared on his face.

"What's happening?" Cindy whispered to Nate.

"I think my mom just put one of your dad's pieces back at the start."

Cindy tried to peer around Nate who was at the door to the den, peeping into the room, most of him hidden so the two adults couldn't see him. "Who's winning?"

"My mom is, but your dad is catching up."

Cindy stood on tiptoes and nearly toppled over. She clutched Nate to steady herself. "I hope your mom wins."

"Why are you two standing here spying?"

Boswell's whispered question caused Cindy to jump. She whirled around and put her finger to her mouth to quiet him. "We don't want them to know we're watching."

Boswell nodded toward the two adults. "I think they know."

Both Nate and Cindy glanced over their shoulders and saw Jesse and Nick watching them with amused looks on their faces.

"Come on in. I'm about to win. All I need is a three." Nick rolled the die and a three came up. He moved his piece the necessary places, then leaped to his feet, high-fiving both Cindy and Nate's hands. "I won. I won."

Frowning, Jesse stared at the board game as though that could change the outcome.

Nick paused in his celebration with the children, sighed and said, "What time do I have to be ready for church? That's the least I can do since I trounced you at Trouble."

Jesse's frown transformed into a full-fledged smile. "Sunday school starts at nine-thirty and church at eleven."

"Church only!" Nick said, a tinge of panic in his voice. He started putting up the game.

"But, Daddy, I want to go to Sunday school with Nate and meet some of his friends. Can't you come to both?"

Jesse thought Cindy had the pout and big eyes routine down pat. She loved the child's slightly bowed head as an added touch. How could Nick say no to that?

"Princess." He looked at his daughter's sad expression and shook his head. "Okay, just this one time."

Cindy threw her arms around his neck and kissed him on the cheek. His smile returned and Jesse felt its full effect. Maybe she should take lessons from the child. She certainly knew how to get to her father.

"Dinner is served, sir," Boswell announced from the doorway.

"Just in time. I've worked up quite an appetite." Jesse put the lid on the Trouble game. "I need my strength for our rematch."

"What rematch? I've had all the Trouble I care to have for the day."

"Do you mean the game or something else?"

"Both. They come in the form of two females."

"Daddy, I'm no trouble." Cindy took his hand and led him toward the kitchen.

"Sweetie, all females are trouble."

"Yeah!" Nate chimed in as he followed them into the kitchen with Jesse next to him.

"I object. We are not." Jesse noticed that Boswell had the food lined up on the counter, buffet-style. The kitchen smelled of cooked ground beef. She loved that aroma. The table was set for five, everything color co-ordinated and matching. She suspected anything Boswell did was done that way. Even the flower arrangement of yellow roses went with the yellow place mats and napkins.

After everyone filled their plates and sat at the table, Jesse said the prayer, making sure she thanked God for getting Nick to agree to come to church, and then they dug into the food. It was a good five minutes before anyone said anything.

"Can I ride with you all tomorrow?" Cindy asked, finishing up her second taco.

"Sure, and your dad can, too. That is, if he wants."

"I think I'd better drive my own car."

He said it so quickly that Jesse couldn't resist teasing him with, "Afraid you'll get trapped at church?"

His hard gaze bore into her for a long moment. "No. Tell you what. I'll drive everyone to church tomorrow. That way we all go together and I'll get to drive my own car."

Jesse started to protest, took a look at the challenge

deep in his eyes and swallowed her words. "That's fine with me. We'll need to leave by eight-thirty."

"I thought Sunday school started at nine-thirty. Isn't it only about a ten-minute drive to the church?" Nick picked up his third taco.

"I have to make coffee for the adult class."

"What are the kids gonna do while you're making coffee? Is there an early service going on at that time?"

"Until a little after nine. But Nate can give you a grand tour of the place or you can always help me make coffee and get all the supplies out."

Cindy downed the last of her chocolate milk and wiped her mouth with her hand. "Can Nate and me go play with Oreo now?"

"Sure, if it's okay with Jesse."

Jesse scanned the kitchen. "Where is Oreo?"

"He's in my bedroom. We have to keep him in there when we're eating. He likes to jump up on the table."

After the children left the kitchen, Boswell began to clean up.

Being the one who always cleaned up at her house, Jesse felt guilty. "Can I help?"

Boswell stopped stacking the dishes and looked at her, his expression neutral. "Madam, this is my job. Thank you for asking, however."

Nick scooted back his chair. "That's our cue to get lost. We can wait for the children in the den."

When Jesse was out of earshot of Boswell, she said, "I don't think I would ever adjust to having a servant full-time. There are too many things I like to do around my house my own way."

"For me it was get help or drown. My wife didn't like to do anything around the house. If I wanted any kind of order in my home, I had to get someone else to do it. Boswell was a lifesaver."

"Did your wife work?"

Nick snorted. "Work! No, not unless you wanted to say she worked at playing hard."

Jesse sat at one end of the brown leather couch while Nick took the other end. She twisted around so she faced him with one cushion between them. "She did a good job with Cindy. She is a precious, polite young lady."

"That wasn't my wife. I can't even say it was me. That was Boswell's doing."

"Is that why you want to spend some time with Cindy this summer? To get to know her?"

"Yes." Nick looked away, his features unreadable. "She's almost seven and I should know my own daughter, but I don't. I was always working, trying to make my company as successful as possible."

"What does success mean to you?"

"Having enough to provide for my family."

"How well do you have to provide before you're satisfied?"

Nick shot to his feet, stiff, his hands curling and uncurling at his sides. "Cindy is never going to know what it's like to want for something to eat or something warm to wear. Never. Not as long as I have a breath in my body."

"But that doesn't seem likely, does it? From what I understand your company is doing very well."

He whirled around, the lines of his face hardening. "But things can change with the snap of a finger. One day I'm healthy, not a care in the world. The next I'm fighting to stay alive and walk again."

"So for you there will never be enough?"

Pacing, Nick prowled his fingers through his hair. "I don't know. I suppose one day there will. Maybe when Cindy is grown-up and making her own way in the world, when I don't have to worry about her."

"As a parent you don't stop worrying just because your child has grown up and moved out. Are you sure you'll be satisfied then?"

He came to a halt in front of her. "I can't answer that. I don't know what the future holds for me. That's my whole point."

"You're right. Life isn't something we can always control. But that can be a wonderful thing, too. If we always know what's going to happen, we can get bored, complacent. This way those little surprises can keep life exciting, keep us on our toes."

"I grew up with no control over my life."

"As a child I didn't have a lot of control over my life, either."

"Maybe a better word is *stability*. You've lived in Sweetwater all your life in a nice house with a whole bunch of people who cared what happened to you."

"Sweetwater takes care of their own."

"No one goes hungry?"

"Not if we know about them."

"I wasn't lucky enough to know a place like Sweetwater."

Jesse's gaze riveted to his. "You do now."

"Why is it important that I attend church with you all tomorrow?"

"I think giving God a chance would help you. Have you ever gone to church?"

He opened and closed his hands. "Yes, when I was growing up. I can remember praying to God for something to eat some nights. It didn't help."

"Are you so sure about that? You're here. You have more than enough now. You didn't die from starvation. Have you ever considered what you went through made you a stronger person? Just because we pray for something doesn't mean we'll get it."

"I wasn't asking for a new toy. I was asking for food or warm clothing. For—" He swallowed hard and turned away.

"For what?"

He stiffened. "Nothing. It doesn't matter now."

"I think it does or you wouldn't have stopped."

Jesse hadn't thought it possible but Nick grew even tenser. She rose and covered the distance between them, placing her hand on his shoulder. Beneath her palm she felt the bunched muscles.

"I'll come to church with you tomorrow because I agreed to it, but that is all. There's nothing there for me anymore."

Jesse's heart broke at the words he uttered. How

could someone turn away from God? From the sacrifice that Jesus made for mankind? "Can Cindy come with us whenever she wants?"

He drew in a deep breath and released it slowly. "If she wants."

"What happens when you return to Chicago? What if she wants to continue attending church?"

He shook his head. "I don't have an answer for you."

The broken pieces of her heart shattered even more until there didn't seem to be anything left. His childhood had been so different from hers. He'd wanted for so much while she had lived a safe, protected life. He blamed God.

Lord, help me to show him the way back to You. How do I help him to see that loving You doesn't guarantee a person an easy life? It only guarantees a person an eternal life in Your kingdom.

"Daddy, come on! We're gonna be late. Jesse needs to get to church to make the coffee."

Nick winced at the loud shouting from his daughter who stood at the bottom of the stairs, probably with her hands on her waist and tapping her foot against the tiled floor. Shoeless, he went to the top step and said, "I'll be down in a minute."

"Hurry. I don't wanna be late for church." Clothed in a pink dress, Cindy danced from foot to foot.

Nick walked back into his bedroom and searched for his brown loafers. *Church.* His memories of church when he was a young boy were vague. His mother would take him each week, spend some extra time praying after everyone left, then come home and cry herself to sleep later that night. Her prayers hadn't helped them. *His* prayers hadn't, either. He'd used to listen to his mother's cries, then get on his knees and offer his own prayer until one day he'd given up trying. What was the use? No one cared. After that he had made a promise to himself. He would only depend on himself. No one else—not even God.

A chill burrowed deep into his bones as he found his shoes and slipped them on his feet. Glancing at himself in the mirror, he noted his casual attire of tan slacks and navy-blue button-down shirt. He was as ready as he would ever be.

Ten minutes later Nick sat behind the steering wheel of his SUV with Jesse next to him and the two children in the back, chatting in lowered voices as though they were telling secrets they didn't want the adults to hear.

Nick tossed his head toward the children. "Should we be worried?"

"Nah. They're just being children."

Tension grew the closer Nick got to the Sweetwater Community Church. His stomach muscles knotted and his palms were sweaty about the steering wheel. The thump of his heart against his chest increased as his breathing quickened.

When he turned into the parking lot at the side of the church, he had begun to force deep breaths into his lungs to slow his bodily functions down. The second he switched off the ignition, Cindy and Nate pushed open the back doors and leaped from the car. He watched them race for the building that must house the Sunday school classes.

Silence reigned in the car, heavy with tension and suppressed emotions.

His white-knuckle grip on the steering wheel under-scored for Jesse the tension that held Nick. She wanted to wipe it away; she wanted to smooth the deep worry lines that carved his features. "You don't have to come in until nine-thirty. I can get the coffee started." She reached out and lay her hand on his arm. The muscles beneath her palm bunched.

"No, I'll help you. I *need* to keep busy."

What had happened to him as a young boy? Jesse wondered when she heard the desperate emphasis on the word *need.* "Sure. I could always use the help. There never seems to be enough time. And speaking of time, we'd better get moving or there'll be no coffee when the first service is over."

As Jesse approached the church with Nick beside her, sounds of the organ and voices singing drifted to them. She angled closer to Nick and took his hand. His cold fingers sent a chill through her that not even the eighty-plus temperature could warm.

He halted by the double doors into the lobby. "I shouldn't have come. This was a mistake."

She could have reminded him of their deal, but she didn't think it would have made any difference. Some-thing from the past gripped him so hard that it gov-erned his actions even today. She pointed toward a garden on the side of the building. "Why don't you sit out there? I can get everything ready. I shouldn't be long."

He stared a long moment at the pine trees in the garden from past Christmases, then focused his attention on her. "You don't mind if I don't help?"

"That wasn't part of the deal. And frankly, you have fulfilled your part of the wager. You have come to church. There wasn't a time allocation of how long you would stay once you came."

Some of the tension in his expression dissolved. Without a word, he wheeled around and headed toward the garden. Jesse slipped inside the building and hurried to the kitchen. Fifteen minutes later she had the coffee made and the supplies laid out on the table. She heard the last hymn being sung as she walked through the lobby and out the double doors.

God would forgive her if she didn't make it to church this morning. She had a more important mission: to discover what had driven Nick away from the Lord.

When she followed the stone path that led to the heart of the garden, she found Nick seated on a bench, his shoulders hunched over, his hands loosely clasped together between spread legs. He stared at the ground at his feet. The tightness around her chest constricted. His body language projected hurt, but she knew when he saw her, his expression would be neutral.

She moved forward. He caught sight of her and lifted his head, his features unreadable. He straightened, even his body conveying nothing of what he was feeling inside.

He glanced at his watch and for a few seconds puzzlement graced his expression.

"I only have to make the coffee. I don't have to serve it. I figured I would keep you company for a while—if that's okay."

He shrugged.

She sat on a bench across from him under the shade of a maple tree, relishing the few degrees of coolness it offered. "Do you want to talk about it?"

"What?"

The defensive tone in his voice cautioned her to move slowly. He wouldn't open up easily if at all. "Your feelings toward the church, God."

He grimaced, looked away.

"Something happened to you. I thought talking about it might help."

"I doubt that."

"When I have a problem, talking about it helps me to work through it."

"That's you."

She inhaled a deep, composing breath. "Has keeping it bottled up inside of you helped?"

His eyes widened for a brief moment then grew narrow as he pinned her with a sharp look. "You deal with your problems one way. I deal with mine another."

"My question still stands. Has it helped to keep everything bottled up inside of you?"

"There isn't much to tell. The church isn't for me. I tried it once. It doesn't meet my needs."

"When? As a child or an adult?"

"Does it matter?" He shot to his feet, his arms stiff at his sides.

"Yes, it matters. How we perceive things as a child is different than we do as an adult."

"If you must know, God let me down." He pivoted away from her, staring through the pine trees toward the parking lot.

"He doesn't promise us a perfect life where everything works out the way we want."

"For years I'd heard about the power of prayer. Well, let me tell you it doesn't work. He doesn't listen."

"He listens. He just doesn't always do what we want. When Mark died, I prayed to Him. I wanted my husband back, but that wasn't going to happen. I did ask Him to help me get through my grief. The Lord was there for me. If it wasn't for Him, I'm not sure what I would have done, especially during the long hours at night when I wanted Mark by my side in bed."

Nick faced her again, his gaze drilling into her. "How do you know the Lord was there for you? You can't see Him."

Chapter Seven

"I know," Jesse whispered, feeling Nick's anguish as though it twisted her insides. "I can't see the wind, either, but I see its effect and know of its existence."

"I've learned to be practical. I don't just take someone's word for something. I need to see it."

She spread her arms wide. "Look around you. Everything you see is God's work. In school I studied photosynthesis and knew God existed. Nothing that complex could randomly exist. Put simply, plants give off oxygen and take in carbon dioxide while we give off carbon dioxide and take in oxygen. What a neat interdependence. Like a marriage, we need each other. That happens a lot in nature. It's the best testimony to the existence of God."

"I wish I had your faith, but it's not that easy."

She held out her hand. "All you have to do is take the first step. Come to church. See for yourself through an adult's eyes. Your perspective might change."

He shook his head. "If anything, I'm much more jaded than I was as a child."

"Perhaps, but you still look at things differently."

He stared at her hand stretched toward him for a long moment, then fit his within her grasp. "I told you I would come to church and I don't back off from a promise even though you were going to graciously let me."

She wasn't going to argue with his reasoning. It was important to her to get him inside to the service. A first step, she hoped, of many more to come.

In the lobby she found Nate with Cindy, talking with Sean and a few of his Sunday school friends. They all surrounded Crystal Bolton in her wheelchair, discussing something the young girl said.

Nate saw her and waved her over. "Mom, Crystal wants to join our basketball team this fall."

"I think that would be a good idea. What does your mom say about it?"

"She said I could try. I saw a special on TV about people in wheelchairs doing all kinds of different sports. Some people with only one leg ski. Others ride horses. Mom would flip out if I wanted to ride a horse. That's why I thought playing basketball would be better. I love to watch the Kentucky Wildcats play."

"What's this about basketball?" Tanya Bolton asked, joining the group.

"I need to get active, Mom. I thought I would play basketball and get a wheelchair that is light and made to do things like that."

Tanya gripped the handles on the back of Crystal's

wheelchair. "We'll talk about it later. Church is about to start."

Jesse saw the shadow of doubt in her friend's eyes. Tanya had just started working after her husband had gone to jail for arson. Money was tight for her, and a new wheelchair would cost a lot of money. She doubted Crystal would get one unless she came up with a way to raise the money. "We'd better get inside, too, Cindy and Nate. Ready?"

The children hurried in front of her and Nick, taking a seat next to Tanya and Crystal, who sat in the aisle in her wheelchair. Tension emanated from Nick as the service started. His actions were stiff as though at any moment he would break into a hundred pieces.

When Reverend Collins began his sermon on the bounty of God's love, Jesse laid her hand over his on the pew between them and smiled. The tight lines about his mouth eased, and he linked his fingers through hers. Through the sermon she noticed that Nick listened to the reverend's words, and after it, he relaxed his tensed muscles and even attempted to sing the last song.

When the congregation began to file out of church, Jesse said, "You have a beautiful voice. Do you sing much?"

"Never," Nick said quickly, as though the mere thought was ridiculous.

"I love to sing, but as you could hear, I wasn't gifted with a beautiful voice."

His gaze trapped hers. "I like your voice."

She blushed. "Are you deaf? Did you not hear me singing right beside you a moment before?"

He chuckled. "You aren't exactly on key, but your speaking voice has a pleasant sound to it."

The color in her cheeks must have flamed even more because she was hot as though the air-conditioning didn't work in the church. "Thank you. I haven't had that compliment before."

"Mom, we're gonna go outside and play. We'll be at the playground."

"Most of the kids go outside after the service while we adults visit inside where it's cool." Jesse watched Cindy and Nate disappear with several other children, Nick's daughter pushing Crystal in her wheelchair. "Cindy has made some friends."

"Usually she's shy."

"Nate won't let her be shy. He doesn't have a shy bone in his body."

"I've noticed. He takes after his mother. I think he knows everyone in town."

"Probably. He's even introduced some people to me."

"No. I don't believe that," Nick said with a laugh, falling into the line of people waiting to say something to the reverend.

"Really." When Jesse reached the front of the line, she said, "Reverend Collins, this is my new neighbor, Nick Blackburn. He and his daughter are here for two months."

The reverend took Nick's hand and shook it. "I'm glad you could visit our church. I met your daughter earlier with Nate. She was telling me how God helped find her little kitten last week."

Surprise flitted into Nick's eyes. "She was hiding in a bush by the lake, and Boswell found her right before he was heading back to the house."

"I enjoyed your sermon today, Reverend Collins."

"The heart of our faith is God's love for his children. It's not that different from the love we have for our own children. Sometimes we have to let them stumble to make them stronger, but that doesn't mean we don't love them."

Nick frowned, his eyebrows slashing downward. "Is that why there is so much suffering in the world?" he asked Jesse as they walked away from the reverend.

"There is evil in this world, Nick. You know that. God is in a constant battle with that evil. People have free will."

"Hey, you two. Jesse, I looked for you before the service. Where did you disappear to?" Darcy asked, joining them in the lobby.

"I wanted to show Nick the garden we planted last year. Even in the heat it's a beautiful place to spend some time."

"It's our meditation garden. I find when things get a little hectic around here it's a good place to escape to for a few minutes."

"This place get hectic? Never!" Jesse saw Joshua weaving his way through the crowd toward his wife. "Nick, this is Darcy's husband, Joshua Markham. They're the ones who teach the summer Sunday school class for the elementary school children. We don't have a regular schedule during the summer."

"I met your daughter this morning," Joshua said after shaking Nick's hand. "She joined the class with Nate and had a lot of good questions. She was very interested in the story of Moses. I hope she comes back again."

Even though Nick was good at hiding his emotions, Jesse could sense his stress. So much was being thrown at him that his system was overloading. "Cindy has an open invitation to come to church with me and Nate. I hate to cut this short but we have to head out."

When Jesse stepped outside, she heard Nick release a long breath. The tension in his expression slipped away. She suspected he was at home in a business environment but a social one was alien to him, especially because this past year he had been recuperating from a series of operations and learning to walk again.

"Thank you," he murmured on the sidewalk in front of the church.

"For what?"

"For understanding. Now where's that playground?" He searched the area.

Perplexed at his half answer, Jesse pointed at the back of the building. "Around on the other side." Mark had always been so easy to read. She had been able to tell what he had been thinking almost before he had. With Nick she was constantly wondering what was going through his head.

As they walked toward the playground, Jesse said, "Darcy and Joshua just got married a few months back.

I'm so happy both of them discovered each other. It was touch-and-go there for a while. Joshua had sworn off ever marrying and Darcy was only here for a few months helping her father run his breeding farm while he was recovering from a heart attack."

"Marriage is fine for some people. I'm just not one of them. Once was enough for me to find that out. I don't make the same mistake a second time. That's one of the reasons I've been so successful in the business world."

"Business and personal lives are two different things."

"Not to me." Nick saw Cindy and waved her over to him.

The young girl ran up to her father, a big smile on her face. "Can I come next week?"

He glanced at Jesse, then placed his hand on Cindy's shoulder. "Sure. Jesse said you could come with her."

"But I want you to come, too. Daddy, you said we would do things together."

His chest expanded with a deep breath that he held for a few seconds before exhaling. "We'll see, sweetie, next week."

"In the meantime, how about you two going fishing with Nate and me? I thought we could have a picnic later," Jesse suggested.

"Yes!" Cindy shouted, jumping up and down and clapping her hands.

"I guess we'll be going fishing," Nick said.

Cindy whirled around and raced toward Nate to tell him.

"I'm sorry. I should have said something before mentioning it in front of Cindy. If you don't want—"

Nick placed his finger over her mouth to stop her flow of words. "I want. It was nice of you to ask us to go with you."

"Nice? Ha! I hate fooling with the bait. I was hoping you would volunteer for the job."

"What do you use?"

"Worms."

"This should be fun."

"I know a sarcastic tone when I hear one. It will be fun."

"If you say so." A smile leaked out, making his eyes glitter with merriment.

"I do."

"I think I'll go with you all and show you the best places to fish." Gramps came into the kitchen while Jesse finished up packing the picnic basket.

She looked up. "I thought you were going over to Susan's house for dinner. Lately you've been going over to see her on Sunday evenings."

"I guess I shouldn't assume anything. She told me she had other plans this evening when I mentioned I would stop by."

"Oh, what's she doing?"

Gramps lifted his shoulders in a shrug, but a frown remained on his face. "Beats me. She didn't say and I asked her straight out. She avoided the question. Most unusual."

"Well, it's not like you two are going steady or anything."

"Yeah, but for the past six weeks we have been doing something together on Sunday *night*. I just thought we would tonight."

"Did you say anything to her before today?"

"No, I didn't think I had to."

Jesse went to the refrigerator and removed some ham and cheese to make her grandfather a sandwich. "You probably should from now on."

"So you think she doesn't have anything to do but is trying to teach me a lesson?"

Removing the bread from the cabinet, Jesse began to put the sandwich together. "Susan doesn't lie. She must have something going on."

He rubbed his chin. "But what? Maybe I should stay here after all and take a long walk this evening."

"Gramps, don't you dare spy on Susan. That wouldn't set well with her if she found out and you know very little is kept a secret for long in Sweetwater."

His shoulders slumped forward. "Fine. I'll tag along with you all."

Jesse wrapped the sandwich in aluminum foil. "Ask her again tomorrow if it bothers you that much."

"I might not see her tomorrow. Two can play hard to get."

Jesse rolled her eyes toward the ceiling, wondering at the games people played, trying to manipulate a situation to their favor. *You're just as guilty, Jesse Bradshaw,* a tiny voice in her mind interjected. She thought about the times she had tried to fix Nick up when he hadn't wanted to be fixed up with a woman. He doesn't want to get married again. He made that very plain this morning at church.

So why am I trying to get him married? The answer to that question was one she was afraid to acknowledge. There was something about Nick that threatened the neat little world she'd created after Mark's death. She had control over this world. She had friends and family whom she loved and who loved her. She had a job she enjoyed. Her emotions were safely wrapped up in her life in Sweetwater. She didn't want to shake up that world.

She was overreacting to the few little stomach flutters and racing heartbeats. Nick and she could be friends. No more trying to fix him up with any female between the age of twenty-five and forty. She could help Cindy while the little girl was in Sweetwater and perhaps even be able to guide Nick back to the Lord.

"Where are you thinking of going?"

Her grandfather's question cut into her musing and pulled her back to the project at hand. "I thought we could fish near where Joe's Creek empties into the lake. That's not too far from here. We can walk there. Hopefully we'll catch some fish."

"I'll let you walk there. I think I'll bring the skiff. Maybe the children will want to fish on the lake."

And leave her and Nick alone. That thought flittered across her mind, along with a sense of panic. She immediately shut down the thought before it took hold. She and Nick were friends. That was all. Even if she had wanted more, he had made it very clear he didn't want a long-term relationship with any woman.

"Fine. We'll meet you over at Joe's Creek." Jesse closed the basket and grabbed the wooden handles to lift.

"I'll take that for you."

The husky sound of Nick's voice caused the back of her neck to tingle. She sucked in a deep breath and almost forgot to breathe. Finally when her lungs screamed for oxygen, she exhaled, then inhaled and released it immediately.

Nick brushed his fingers over the back of her hand holding the basket as he took it from her. "What do you have in here? Your whole kitchen?"

"Just a few things to eat for dinner. Fishing can make a person mighty hungry."

"I agree. Lifting those fishing rods can be taxing."

"You just wait. You'll be glad I brought this food. Where's Cindy?"

"Nate let us in and he wanted to show her something in his room."

"Is Boswell coming?"

"No, he had something to do."

"He shouldn't stay cooped up in the house. It's a beautiful day."

Nick cocked his head and scrunched his mouth into a thoughtful expression. "You know, I don't think he's staying home. I got the impression he was going somewhere."

"We're ready." Nate appeared in the doorway with Cindy and Bingo beside him.

Gramps headed for the back door. "I'll take the fishing equipment in the skiff."

"Can we go with you, Gramps?" Nate hurried across the room with Cindy and Bingo trailing behind him.

Her grandfather paused and peered back at Jesse. "Is that okay with you two? I can even take that basket."

"Only if the children wear a life jacket."

"Ah, Mom, I can swim."

"You know my rule. When you're in the boat, you have to wear a life jacket."

"Fiiinne."

Nick and she followed her grandfather and the children down to the pier, skirting the area where Fred and Ethel were with their baby geese. Nick helped Cindy put on her life jacket then he deposited the basket in the bottom of the skiff. By the time the fishing equipment and the three passengers were in the small boat, there was no more room for anything or anyone else.

After Nick untied the ropes, Gramps started the motor and the skiff slowly left the dock. "See you two at Joe's Creek. Don't get lost in the woods."

Jesse could hear Cindy say, "The woods? I don't want Daddy to get lost."

Her grandfather's booming laugh sounded in the quiet afternoon air. Then Nate explained to Cindy how small the woods around Joe's Creek was.

"Do you think they'll be all right?" Nick asked, frowning as he watched the skiff head toward the shoreline to the east.

"Yes. I'd never have let Nate go if I thought otherwise. Don't worry."

"Easier said than done. I used to not worry about Cindy. Now I do all the time. After my accident I realized how precarious life can be, how quickly it can change."

"Life is a series of changes. Nothing stays the same for long." Jesse heard her own words and realized how much she had been trying to keep her life the same, too.

"So how long is this walk to Joe's Creek?"

"Oh, about a mile. Not too far."

"Speak for yourself."

Even though his tone was teasing, Jesse remembered Nick's bad leg and said, "There's a road that is about three or four hundred yards away from where we're gonna fish. We can drive if you want."

Nick massaged the top of his right thigh. "I'll be fine. I need to walk more. When I return to Chicago, I want this leg one hundred percent."

Jesse moved down the pier. "You miss being in Chicago?"

"I miss working. I conduct some of it from here, but I promised Cindy and myself I would take some time off so I'm trying to minimize the amount of time I work while in Sweetwater. But for so many years work is what has defined who I am. That's not easy to walk away from."

"But you aren't walking away from it. You still have your work. It'll be there when you go back." Jesse noticed that Fred kept a wary eye on them as they avoided the area where the flock of geese grazed in the tall grass by the lake.

"I've done such a good job of hiring capable managers that the company is practically running itself."

"And that bothers you?"

"The last few years of my marriage to Brenda, I knew she didn't need me. But my company did. Or so I thought. Now I know I was kidding myself."

"So what are you going to do when you get back?"

"I'll get Cindy settled in school, then…" He paused. "I don't know. I haven't decided. I do know I need to spend more time with Cindy when we get back."

"You have a wonderful daughter."

"Each day I am discovering just how wonderful. This afternoon she asked me if we could help get Crystal a new wheelchair so she could play basketball. She offered the money she had been saving."

"That's so sweet, but I'm not sure Tanya wants Crystal doing that."

"If she decides to, I would be glad to buy the wheelchair."

"You would?"

"I have plenty of money. I give a certain amount every year to different causes. It would be nice knowing who will benefit."

"Then some good things are coming out of your visit to Sweetwater."

He didn't say anything about her comment concerning Sweetwater, and she wondered if he regretted coming to spend a couple of months in the house next to hers. Her community wasn't like Chicago at all.

Jesse, my girl, what did you want him to say? That Sweetwater was the perfect place to live? That he couldn't think of any place better to be? She shook her head as if that could rid herself of that little voice in the back of her mind.

When Bingo ran ahead of them yelping, she realized they were near Joe's Creek and the others. She could hear Nate and Cindy laughing while Gramps grumbled, his words too low to make out what he was saying.

She and Nick stepped out of the shadow of the trees that ran along the creek and found Gramps trudging toward shore, pulling the rope attached to the skiff.

Nate saw them. He began to laugh even more, pointing to his great-grandfather. "He didn't tie the boat up good enough. It started drifting away. He had to run after it before it ended up in the middle of the lake."

"He was funny splashing in the water." Cindy continued to laugh beside Nate.

With water dripping off him, Gramps grumbled some more, bent down and tied the skiff again, checking to make sure the rope wouldn't slip free. "You two distracted me."

"Welcome to a Bradshaw picnic," Jesse whispered to Nate. "Sure you want to stay?"

"Isn't laughter supposed to be the best medicine?" he asked, chuckling at the loud sloshing sound Gramps made with his wet tennis shoes as he headed back to the boat to retrieve the last of the fishing equipment.

Nick leaned back against an oak tree, resting his arm on a knee. "Are there any more cookies left?"

"Nope. Cindy and Nate finished off the last two before leaving with Gramps to head back home."

"That's what I thought, but I was hoping a couple or three slipped down inside the basket." The back of his head touched the rough bark of the tree as his eyes slid closed, and he relished the quiet of the moment. A bird chirped above him. A person more used to the woods would probably know what kind of bird. He had to admit he had rarely spent time in the country and this was certainly an experience.

"Did you enjoy fishing even though you didn't catch anything?"

Jesse's question brought a smile to his lips. "Seeing you try to bait your hook was well worth the time spent trying to fish."

"*You* were supposed to bait my hook for me."

"But your grandfather insisted you do it yourself. I was taught never to go against my elders."

Jesse snorted. "At least I caught a fish. And Nate. And Gramps. And Cindy."

"Yeah, did you see her big smile when she pulled in that fish?"

Jesse finished putting the trash and leftover food into the basket. "It's called a crappie. She enjoyed herself."

"And so did I." Pushing to his feet, Nick took the blanket he had been sitting on and began folding it. "Anytime you want to ask Cindy and I to come fishing please feel free to."

"I can loan you a couple of rods and reels so you and Cindy can go anytime you want."

"I'll see what she says, but I think she liked the skiff the most."

"Has she ever been in a boat?"

"She went on a friend's yacht on Lake Michigan once. Not quite the same experience. I'm not even sure she realized she was on the water. She stayed in the cabin and watched TV the whole time." Nick took the basket and started toward the trail they'd used earlier.

The "woods" were no more than twenty or thirty trees of various kinds that flanked one side of the creek. In less than three minutes he and Jesse emerged from the woods and saw their houses in the distance. Gramps docked the skiff at the pier behind Jesse's home. The children ran ahead of the old man toward Jesse's deck.

Nick looked toward the lake, glass smooth. The sun had sunk below the tree line to the west, and the sky was ribboned with oranges and reds. He drew in a deep breath saturated with the scent of forest and earth. "It's a gorgeous day," he murmured, surprised by the feeling of contentment that held him.

Stepping over a log, Jesse slipped and nearly fell. Nick quickly dropped the basket and grabbed for her. Steadying her, he brought her up against him. Her jasmine scent chased away all others. He filled his nostrils with it, closing his eyes for a few seconds as he savored having a beautiful woman in his arms.

Then the fact he was holding Jesse registered, and he quickly let her go, moving back a few paces while he picked up the basket.

But the rapid rise and fall of her chest attested to the effect their encounter had on her. Something more than friendship could develop between them if he allowed it. It wasn't fair of him to take this any further. He would be gone in a month's time and Jesse deserved more than that. She deserved a husband like her first one, who would love her totally and be committed to a relationship that would last a lifetime. He had learned the hard way he wasn't that kind of man. He wouldn't make that mistake again.

"That's funny." Jesse frowned. "Where's Gramps going?"

Nick followed the direction Jesse pointed and saw the older man hurrying toward the house he rented. Jesse's grandfather still clutched the cooler with the fish they had caught. The way he held himself suggested one angry man. "My house? Why?"

"Oh, no. Look."

Boswell brought two tall glasses outside and handed one to a woman. "Who is that?"

"I think it's Susan Reed and Gramps isn't a happy camper. We'd better hurry and intercede." She hastened her steps.

"Unless we can fly we won't make it in time."

Nick watched Jesse's grandfather come to halt in front of Boswell who sat next to Susan on the deck. The old man's shouts could probably be heard in town or across the lake.

"Oh, my." Jesse began to jog.

As Nick and Jesse approached the trio, Nate and Cindy stood between Gramps and Boswell with Susan off to the side wringing her hands and shaking her head.

"So this was why you didn't come with us fishing. Trying to horn in on my gal."

"Gerard Daniels, I am not your gal."

"Yes, you are." Gramps flicked a glance toward

Susan before returning his steely look to Boswell, almost toe to toe with him.

"No, I am not. I invited Boswell to experience a good American dinner at my house."

This time Jesse's grandfather turned his full attention to Susan. "*You* invited him? On *our* night?"

Jesse stepped forward before a war erupted on Nick's deck. "Nate, why don't you show Cindy your snake?"

"She's seen it," Nate replied as though there wasn't anything that could possibly drag him away from the action.

"Nate!"

Except the warning tone in his mother's voice, Nick thought with amusement.

"Oh, all right." Nate huffed. "I don't see why I have to show her something she's already seen."

"Daddy?" His daughter whined, clearly not wanting to leave either if her eager expression was any indication.

"Go on, Cindy. We'll be over in a minute."

Nate and Cindy stomped off, whispering between themselves, while Jesse's grandfather pressed his lips together and glared at Susan.

When the children were inside Jesse's house, her grandfather said, "Well, what do you have to say for yourself, Susan Reed?"

Susan returned his glare, folding her arms across her chest. "Absolutely nothing. I'm going home, Gerard Daniels. Alone." She swung to Boswell, smiled at him and said, "Thank you for a lovely evening. I'll see your stamp collection another time."

"I'll walk you to your car."

Susan shook her head. "I can find my own way. But thanks, anyway."

When she was gone, Jesse's grandfather moved to block Boswell's path into the house. "Stamp collection? When trying to lure a woman home, couldn't you come up with something better than that?"

Boswell straightened his shoulders and looked down his nose at Jesse's grandfather. "I would put my stamp collection up against anyone else's around here. I have some rare stamps."

"I just bet you do. Is that what you told Susan to get her to come back here after dinner?"

Boswell puffed out his chest. "What I say to Susan is none of your business. Now if you will kindly move, I am retiring for the evening." He didn't wait for Jesse's grandfather to step aside. He pushed past him and was inside the sliding glass doors before Gramps could recover and say anything.

He stood staring at Boswell's retreating back, clenching and unclenching his hands. "Well, I never," he muttered.

Jesse lay her hand on Gramps's shoulder. "You'd better clean the fish before they spoil."

Gramps frowned. "I don't understand Susan anymore. Why would she go out with him?" He flicked his wrist toward the sliding glass door.

"Gramps, have you ever talked to Susan about how you feel?"

He stared at her as though she had suddenly sprouted

a second head. "Why would I do that? I'm not good with words. She should know how I feel."

"A woman likes to hear a man tell her. Don't expect her to read your mind."

He whirled about and stalked toward Jesse's house. "I've got fish to clean. The rods and reels are still on the pier. I don't have time to tell a woman how I feel."

Jesse's posture seemed to deflate.

"Are you all right, Jesse?" Nick touched her arm.

She jerked away as though surprised to find him there. For a few seconds her weariness lined her face then gradually a smile transformed it into a picture of serenity. "Yes. Gramps sometimes takes an extra dose of my patience, but I love him."

He held out his hand to her. "Come on. I'll help you get the fishing equipment. I want to get my half of the fish, too."

"Half! I don't recall you catching half."

The fit of her hand within his comforted him. He began walking toward the pier. "But I was hoping you would take pity on a novice and give me more than my share."

"Tell you what. I'll do one better. We'll have a fish fry tomorrow night and you, Boswell and Cindy are invited."

"Are you sure about Boswell and Gramps being together?"

"They're two grown men and they'll have to learn to behave around each other."

"Just because you declare it doesn't mean it will happen."

"I'll have a talk with Gramps and point out the fact young ears will be listening. That usually works."

The growing darkness cloaked him in a sense of well-being. Even though his leg ached and he found himself limping more profoundly, being next to Jesse made the pain insignificant. The sound of the water lapping against the pier calmed him. The fresh scent of nature soothed his senses. But most of all, Jesse's presence pacified the restlessness within.

At the end of the pier where the rods and reels lay, Nick paused, turning toward Jesse. The shadows of dusk didn't hide her smile. The gleam in her eyes drew him a step closer. Linking both hands with hers, he laced their fingers and brought them up between them.

The pounding of his heart drove all rational sense from his mind as he leaned toward her.

Chapter Eight

Nick paused. A whisper separated Jesse from him. If she moved even an inch, their lips would touch. Her heartbeat kicked up a notch, thumping against her rib cage so loudly she wondered if he could hear it.

Releasing her hands, he brought his up to cup her face, so lovingly she wanted to melt against him. His gaze linked to hers as their fingers had been only seconds before, a tangible connection.

"You are so beautiful."

His softly spoken compliment robbed her of coherent thought. She stood before him mesmerized by his eyes, dark pools that reflected a painful past, an inner struggle. He fought to mask his expression but she saw his anguish, hidden from most.

"Today was fun."

She latched on to his comment as though it were a lifeline. "Yes, it was." Her mouth dry, she licked her lips. "Nate got a kick out of showing you how to fish."

He grinned, tiny lines fanning out from his eyes. "I noticed your grandfather laughing a few times at my poor attempt to cast a line."

"That's why they tolerate me. I'm great at untangling lines."

"I noticed."

The space between them shrunk. Their breaths tangled. His hands combed through her short hair and pressed her closer. His mouth settled over hers, and she thought the world had stopped spinning. She clung to him and savored the feel of his lips as they moved over hers.

When he pulled back, she realized she was losing her battle to remain detached. She cared about Cindy, but she also cared about Nick—too much. They lived in different worlds. His revolved around his work in Chicago. Hers revolved around her faith and Sweetwater and that wasn't going to change. She didn't see any way for their two worlds to mesh together.

Quickly before she lost her nerve, she stepped back. "Why did you do that?" *Why did you make me care about you?*

His brows slashed downward. "I don't know why. It seemed the right thing to do at the time." Moving away even farther, Nick bent and picked up the rods and reels, cradling them in his arms.

"I consider you a friend."

"I feel the same way."

"But that is all. There is no future in anything else."

A frown carved his features with harsh lines. "It was just a kiss, Jesse. I agree there is no future for us. You're the marrying kind and I don't want to get married."

His words hurt. "I don't, either. Besides, you live in Chicago and I live here. I won't leave Sweetwater. My life is here." Her voice rose a level.

"My life is in Chicago," Nick said in a near shout.

She placed her fists on her waist and glared at him. "I like a quiet, simpler life."

He started to say something, stopped and snapped his mouth closed. Then he chuckled. "Actually I'm beginning to value quiet and simple," he whispered, scanning the area.

The tension siphoned from Jesse. She didn't normally blow up at a person for no reason and a kiss wasn't really a good reason. "Sorry. I think I overreacted. You took me by surprise."

"I took myself by surprise. It was a nice kiss, though."

Something inside of her melted as she thought back to the kiss. "Yes, it was."

"Still friends?"

She nodded.

"Good." He released a long sigh. "Because Cindy adores you."

"And Nate adores you."

"I'm thinking about seeing if the Millers will sell this house. I'd like to buy it and use it as a summer home."

His declaration shocked her. Her mouth parted but no words came out. He would return each summer! The mere thought sent her mind whirling, her pulse rate speeding.

"I haven't said anything to Cindy yet so I would appreciate it if you wouldn't. I'm not sure if I will, but this is a good place for her. We both could use some down time where it is quiet and we can regroup as a family."

Jesse heard his explanation, but the words didn't really register. She was still trying to work through the fact she would see him every summer—just long enough to begin to care—whoa! She wasn't going to go there. If he did buy the house, she would deal with it when it occurred.

"What do you think?"

"I think Sweetwater is a good place for Cindy. She has already made some friends, and Nate will be excited if you come back every summer."

"And you?"

Oh, dear, why did he have to ask that question? "Of course," she finally answered, her throat thick with emotions she was trying to deny.

"It's important to get along with your neighbors. There isn't anyone on the left and with you on the right I know this would be a good place."

"You can say that after what we witnessed earlier between Gramps and Boswell?"

"I guess I'd better get Boswell's opinion. He's invaluable and I wouldn't want to lose him."

"Gramps can have that effect on people. I really don't blame Susan for looking elsewhere. She and Gramps have been dating on and off for several years. She's wanted to take the relationship to the next level and my grandfather has been dragging his feet. Commitment shy."

"I can understand that."

"Here, let me help you with those rods."

"Nah, I've got them." He glanced about. "I guess we'd better head to the house. It's almost completely dark."

She hadn't noticed how dark it had become. The light at the end of the pier that automatically came on gave off enough illumination that she could see Nick's face. But the surrounding landscape was obscured as though someone had thrown a dark blanket over them, shielding them in their own world.

"I'm surprised that Nate and Cindy haven't come out to see where we are." Jesse began walking toward the end of the pier.

Nick fell into step next to her. "They're probably quizzing your grandfather about what happened."

"I hadn't thought about that. We'd better hurry. No telling what he will tell them." She quickened her pace.

Nick placed the rods and reels down by the back door. When Jesse entered the kitchen, she found Nate, Cindy and Gramps sitting at the table, drinking sodas and eating some oatmeal cookies. She thought of the caffeine in the sodas and groaned.

"Gramps, Nate isn't supposed to have a soda this late."

"So upset, it must have slipped my mind."

Nate quickly downed the rest of his can. "I'll go to bed on time."

"But will you go to sleep on time?"

"Sure." Her son flashed her a grin, popped the last bit

of cookie into his mouth and leaped to his feet. "Come on, Cindy. I'm going to feed my animals. Wanna help?"

"Yes." Cindy grabbed her last cookie and stuffed it into her mouth as they raced from the room.

"I guess I'll be leaving, too." Gramps pushed himself to his feet and scooped up the remaining cookies to take with him.

Jesse stared at the mess left on the kitchen table, crumbs, empty pop cans. "What just happened here?"

"I think it's called fleeing the scene of the crime."

"We'll be lucky if they go to sleep before three in the morning. They have enough sugar and caffeine in them for ten kids." Jesse retrieved a dishcloth from the sink and wiped off the table.

Nick tossed the cans into the recycling bin. "When Cindy doesn't sleep, I don't sleep."

"That's being a full-fledged parent. Never rest unless your child is resting. I've worked on many a doll in the middle of the night. Not a bad time to read, either."

"I'll keep that in mind when I'm up tonight. Better yet, I'll call you and you can keep me company."

"Sure," she said, not really thinking he would.

But six hours later Jesse answered the phone on the first ring, nearly jumping out of the chair she sat in. "Hello," she said breathlessly.

"Hi. I thought you'd be up, and when I saw your light on in the den, I figured I would take you up on keeping me company."

"Nick?" she asked, knowing full well it was him.

"Who else would be calling you this late?"

Jesse glanced at the clock. "It's three!" She had been so busy on her latest doll for the Fourth of July auction at church that she had lost track of time.

"Very good."

"Cindy's still up?"

"No, she went to bed hours ago."

"Then why are you up?"

"Couldn't sleep. I guess all that talk about not sleeping put the suggestion in my brain. Is Nate still up?"

She listened for any sound coming from upstairs. His room was right above the den. "No, I guess he's finally gone to sleep. You know, I could have been Gramps. He doesn't always sleep well."

"I saw you through the window."

Jesse lifted her head and stared at the darkness outside. She often forgot to draw the drapes. Rising, she walked to the window and looked toward Nick's house. With a phone to his ear, he watched her. She waved. He waved back.

"You really should pull your curtains."

"This isn't Chicago."

"I know. Every day I am reminded of how different Sweetwater is from Chicago." He moved away from the window. "What are you doing? You look so intense working at that table."

"Making a doll for the church benefit."

"When is it? I might have to buy it. I know Cindy would want an original doll by Jesse."

"It's for an auction and it's on the Fourth of July. The money goes toward our outreach program so I

hope you will come and force the bidding up high."
She missed seeing him in the window. Reluctantly
Jesse pulled the drapes, then returned to her chair at the
card table.

"You've got yourself a date," Nick's deep raspy voice
came through the receiver.

The word *date* sent a shiver down her spine. She
clutched the phone tighter to her ear and squeezed her
eyes shut for a few seconds, reliving the *kiss*. Her mouth
tingled. "Maybe Cindy would like to help me make a
doll she can donate to the auction."

"I'll ask her. And while you keep my daughter enter-
tained, I'll take your son fishing. I went online when I
couldn't sleep and got some information about fishing that
should help me. I'm determined to catch one this time."

"Sure. We can add them to the fish fry."

"Sounds good to me."

She heard him yawn and yawned herself. "We'd better get some sleep or we won't be much good tomorrow."

"Sweet dreams, Jesse."

She sat for a long moment, her hand lingering on the
receiver, visualizing Nick in his house, dressed comfort-
ably, with a lazy smile on his face and a dancing gleam
in his eyes, his feet propped up on an ottoman. At home.
In Sweetwater.

She sighed and wiped the picture from her mind.
Too dangerous.

Jesse sat at the kitchen table with her hand cupping
her chin and her elbow on the wooden surface. Her eye-

lids began to slide closed even though Nate and Gramps were talking—had been nonstop for the past fifteen minutes. The drone of their voices lulled her to sleep—sleep she should have gotten the night before. Even when she went to bed, she'd tossed about on her mattress as though she were a small boat on an ocean caught in a big storm. And at the center of the storm was Nick Blackburn!

"Mom!"

Nate shook her shoulder, rousing her from her dreamlike state. She straightened, blinking. "What?"

"You weren't listening to what I said."

"I'm afraid I didn't get enough sleep last night. A little boy was up way too late and kept me up, too."

Nate dropped his head. "Sorry, Mom."

"That's okay, sweetheart."

His head shot back up, and he grinned from ear to ear. "Did you hear? Nick's taking me fishing this morning. Isn't that great?"

"Wonderful, darling." Jesse took a large swallow of her lukewarm coffee, hoping the caffeine would kick in real soon before she laid her head on the table and started snoring.

"He wants me to give him some more pointers on how to fish. Me, Mom," Nate pointed to himself. "Can you believe it?"

She ruffled her son's hair. "Yes. You're a good fisherman."

"You need to take the skiff to O'Reilly's Cove," Gramps advised as he stood and shuffled toward the coffeepot to pour himself some more of the brew. "Should be some fish there. All he should have to do is put his line in the water to catch anything." He lifted the glass pot toward Jesse.

"Yes, please." She slid her mug with painted lady-bugs on it across the table, then slid it back when her grandfather refilled it to the brim. Steam wafted to the ceiling, the rich dark color reminding Jesse of Nick's eyes. Why was it everywhere she turned she thought of Nick? "I think Gramps is right. O'Reilly's Cove has some of the best fishing on the lake."

"Gramps, it's okay if we take the skiff then?"

"Sure, son. I've got some powerful thinking to do today so I won't be using it." Gramps eased back into his chair, cradling his mug between his hands.

"Thinking?" both Nate and Jesse said at the same time.

"Every once and a while a man's got to do some thinking about his life. Take stock of the direction it's heading. You'll learn that as you grow up."

Jesse wasn't sure one hundred percent her grandfather was just talking to Nate. There was a look in his eyes that said his comments were also aimed at her. She didn't see any need to change the direction her life was heading. She was content with it the way it was. And everything will be back to normal when Nick and Cindy leave in a month, she declared silently.

She repositioned herself in her chair, trying to get comfortable. Again she found herself staring at the coffee in the mug and thinking about the man next door. He should be here soon. How did she look? She'd been so tired when she had gotten up that she hadn't even looked in the mirror when she'd combed her hair.

A knock at the back door sent Nate leaping from his chair and hurrying to answer it. The man who had plagued her thoughts appeared in the entrance with a smile on his face but tired lines about his eyes. Good, he hadn't gotten any more sleep than she had, and it was affecting him, too.

"Ready to go after Moby Dick?" Nick stepped into the house with Cindy right behind him, eating a piece of toast with strawberry jam.

"Moby Dick?" Nate asked, his face screwing up into a confused expression.

"A whale in a story I once read."

"There aren't any whales in the lake." Nate whirled toward his great-grandfather. "Are there, Gramps?"

"No, son. He was just kidding."

"Oh." Nate turned back to Nick and said in a serious tone, "There is an old catfish that Gramps keeps trying to catch. He's pretty slippery. He lives in O'Reilly's Cove. Maybe you can get him."

"Or maybe you can." Nick saw the coffeepot still half full. "May I have a cup before we hit the water?"

"Yes." Jesse rose and went to the counter to pour Nick a mug. "Are you ready to help me make a doll, Cindy?"

Still chewing the last of her toast, the little girl nodded.

Nick leaned against the counter and sipped his coffee. "The second she heard about the plans for today, she grabbed the last piece of toast on her plate and dragged me out the door. I didn't even get to finish my coffee. So this is a welcomed relief." He raised his mug.

"Did you get anything to eat? I could fix you something."

Nick shook his head. "I'm fine. Coffee is all I need right now. How far is this O'Reilly's Cove? Do we walk or drive?"

"You can use the skiff. Much easier." Gramps stood and brought his cup to the sink, then headed toward the door.

"Why don't you come with us, sir?"

Before disappearing out the back door, Gramps glanced over his shoulder. "Thanks, but I've got plans."

When her grandfather closed the door, Nick asked, "He isn't going over to my house to see Boswell, is he?"

Jesse walked to the window to watch her grandfather head away from Nick's house. "No, I don't think so. He likes to walk when he has some thinking to do. I wouldn't be surprised if he turns up at O'Reilly's Cove later."

Nate tried to whistle but didn't quite make the correct sound. "That's far."

"Are you ready to leave?" Nick finished the last of his coffee and placed the mug on the counter by the sink. "I saw the fishing equipment on the deck by the door."

"Gramps checked to make sure we had everything."

"You'd better get your ball cap. It's gonna be hot in a few hours." As Nate and Cindy left the kitchen in search of his hat, Jesse said, "Make sure he puts on sunscreen every hour. He tends to burn easily if he doesn't. And he will have to wear a life jacket. He'll complain."

Nick's gaze captured hers. "I'll take good care of him. Like he was my own." After he said the last sentence, Nick's eyes widened for a few seconds, then he turned away so Jesse couldn't see his expression.

But his words stuck in her mind and played through her thoughts as she watched her son and neighbor walk down to the pier and get into the skiff. Even when working with Cindy to make a small baby doll for the auction, she couldn't keep from thinking about Nick. What were he and Nate doing right that moment? Had they caught a fish yet? Were they having a good time?

"Jesse. Jesse." Cindy's voice pulled her from her thoughts. She shook the image of Nick seated in the skiff steering it toward the calmer water of the cove. "Sorry, I was thinking about a…friend."

"Is this enough stuffing for the arms?"

"I'd use a little more." Jesse rose from her worktable in the den and walked toward the window.

The sparkling blue water gleamed in the sunlight. She looked toward the direction of O'Reilly's Cove, wondering what Nate and Nick were doing. Maybe Cindy and she should drive around to the cove and try to spot them. She could use a break and she was sure Cindy could, too.

"Want to check out what your dad and Nate are doing?" Jesse rolled her shoulders to work the stiffness out of them.

"Daddy didn't eat any breakfast. Maybe we could bring them something to eat."

"What a wonderful idea." Jesse walked to Cindy and hugged the child. "Your father is lucky to have you as a daughter."

"Boswell says he needs me."

"And I agree with Boswell. What do you think we should bring them to eat?"

Cindy laid the arms to her doll on the table and stood. "Daddy likes ham or turkey sandwiches."

"Great. I've got some turkey and I'll fix a peanut butter and jelly one for Nate. Do you want one, too?"

"Yes."

In the kitchen with Cindy's help Jesse had the sandwiches prepared in ten minutes. She took several sodas from the refrigerator and a bag of cookies from the pantry and placed the food and drinks in a big paper sack.

"Ready." Jesse grabbed her set of keys and started for the back door.

Fifteen minutes later she and Cindy stood on the shore at O'Reilly's Cove and waved at Nick and Nate in the skiff out in the middle about thirty yards away. When her son saw them, he got to his feet, waving back at them. The skiff rocked in the water. Nick gripped Nate's hand and yanked him back down on the seat.

The sound of the motor echoed through the tree-lined cove. Nick directed the skiff toward them and shore. The second he landed the boat on the small sandy beach, Nate jumped from it and splashed through the shallow water toward them.

"I'm sure glad Gramps didn't see you standing up in the boat. Now you see why I have you wear a life jacket."

"Don't tell Gramps I forgot."

"No more complaining about wearing a life jacket."

"Promise."

"Finished the doll already?" Nick asked Cindy, appearing at Nate's side.

"Almost, Daddy. I've got all the parts done. We just have to put it together."

"We thought we would take a break and bring you guys something to eat. Hungry?"

"Yep. What you got?" Nate peered into the sack that Jesse held.

She gave him the bag. "Sandwiches, sodas and cookies. Nothing fancy."

"I'm starved. My kind of lunch—food." Nick said, checking out the sack's contents, too.

Jesse chuckled. "You wouldn't be so hungry if you didn't skip breakfast. It's the most important meal of the day."

"Have you been talking to Boswell? That's what he says."

"Nope. Know that fact all on my own."

Nate took the sack to an outcrop of rocks and put it down on a flat one that resembled a stone table. Both her son and Nick delved inside and withdrew the contents, Nate licking his lips while Nick's eyes gleamed in appreciation.

"Fishing is hard work. I could eat double this." Nick unwrapped his sandwich and took a big bite.

"All you've done is sit around waiting for a fish to take the bait. That isn't hard work in my book. By the way, do you have any?"

Nick shook his head while chewing his second bite.

After washing his food down with a swallow of pop, he said, "Worrying is hard work."

"What in the world are you worrying about?"

"When or even *if* I'm gonna catch a fish."

Jesse stepped away from the children who sat on the rocks, eating peanut butter and jelly sandwiches. "You're really getting into this fishing."

"I've got a reputation to uphold."

"What reputation?"

"Whatever I set my mind to, I do well."

"Then I've got confidence you will conquer fishing…one day."

"I hear doubt in your voice that it won't be today."

"There's more to fishing than just putting your line in the water and getting a fish."

"I know that."

"You can't conquer it in one day. Gramps has been doing it for years, and he's still amazed at some of the things that have happened."

"Like the old catfish that has evaded him?"

"I personally hope he never catches it. It gives him something to look forward to each time he goes out."

"And we need something to look forward to when we wake up each morning."

"Yes. I thank God every day I get out of bed."

"Why? He took the one person you loved the most away from you."

The harsh tone of Nick's voice took her by surprise. His words snatched her breath. She couldn't think of anything to say for a long moment. Then an answer came into her mind as though God spoke to her. "Mark is with the Lord now. One day I will join him so he's not lost to me. My memories of my husband will sustain me until then." She tilted her head. "Why are you angry with God?"

"If He loves us so much, why do we suffer?"

"He's never denied us free will. We have choices. Sometimes they lead to heartache. As a parent, do you not find there are times you must discipline your child? That is the way children learn."

"Gramps!"

Nate's shout drew Jesse's attention. Her grandfather strode across the beach toward them.

"I was nearby and thought I would see how you two were doing. Caught any fish yet?"

"No," both Nick and Nate answered at the same time.

"Nick got a nibble and I think I lost the old catfish. He snapped my line. I had to show Nick how to fix it."

"I half expected you to be here when I showed up. What took you so long, Gramps?" Jesse asked, seeing the intensity in Nick's features smooth into a neutral expression.

"I made a little stop on the way." Her grandfather stared at the ground, toeing the sand at his feet.

"Did Susan see you?"

His head shot up. "No. I know she was home. Her car was in the driveway, but she wouldn't open the door to me."

"Do you blame her after your antics last night?"

"That's okay. I'll catch her when we're setting up for

the Fourth of July celebration. She won't miss that. She'll have to talk to me then."

"Daddy, can we help set up, too? Jesse told me they could always use extra people." Cindy hopped down from her rock to come stand by her father. "They spend all day the day before getting everything ready."

When Nick didn't answer immediately, Jesse said, "If you have something to do, Cindy can go with us. Her doll will be on display on a table until the auction."

"No, I'm pretty free until the end of July. What time?"

"We have breakfast together at seven, then there's an early morning worship service for the helpers, then we start setting up. The service is at eight. We will probably be putting things out by nine. You can always meet us there at nine."

"Daddy, Jesse needs me to help with breakfast. She's in charge of it. Can we go at seven?"

Chapter Nine

Nick looked from his daughter to Jesse, feeling trapped. He couldn't deny Cindy her request but that meant they would stay for the service at eight. Ever since the one he had attended with Jesse, he hadn't been able to get the reverend's words out of his mind. They haunted him with memories of his past, attending church with his mother every week until she was too ill to go. She died a broken woman, her hard life dragging her down until she couldn't get up anymore.

"Daddy, can we?"

"Sure, sweetie. We can help."

Cindy clapped and hurried back to Nate on the rocks. She grabbed a cookie and stuffed it into her mouth, then finished her soda. Gramps joined them, taking a cookie from the bag.

"Will you be all right with going at seven?"

"You mean can I deal with attending a church service? Yes. It's important to Cindy."

"You know Cindy is right. I could use a few extra pair of hands to help with breakfast."

"What time do you need us there?"

"Six or six-thirty, whenever you can make it."

"The day is getting longer and longer. When do you usually finish getting everything ready?"

"Oh, about five or so. It depends on how many times we stop to chat."

"I'm thinking the setup is one big social event."

"Almost more than the actual Fourth of July celebration."

Nick turned to Nate. "Are you ready to fish some more?"

"Yep. Gramps is gonna ride back with us in the skiff."

"We might be a while. I'm determined to catch a fish." Nick began walking toward the boat, his leg aching.

Gramps put an arm about his shoulder. "Son, fishing happens in its own time frame. Just because you want it doesn't mean it will happen today. But I can give you some pointers to help your cause."

Nick pushed the skiff out into the water, took his seat and started the motor. He waved goodbye to Jesse and Cindy. He'd been pleased to see them earlier and hated seeing them leave. But he and Nate had some serious fishing to do. Despite what Gramps said, he intended to catch himself a fish today.

"You want me to be in charge of the bacon? Have you gone daft?" Nick asked standing in the middle of the church kitchen. "You remember what I nearly did to the fish at the fish fry the other night. Charred is not one of my favorite ways to eat fish or bacon."

With wooden spoon in hand, Jesse placed her fists on her waist. "Darcy called and told me she's running late. She was supposed to help me cook."

"How about one of the other ladies?"

"Beth's taking care of the biscuits, Zoey the gravy and I'm doing the eggs. You can trade places with any of us." When he didn't say anything, she continued, "Here let me show you how, using the microwave. It's about a minute for each piece of bacon." Using a paper plate and paper towels, Jesse stacked six pieces, then punched in the time. "All you have to do is get it out, check to make sure they're done enough, then repeat the process."

"I can do that." Relieved, Nick moved in front of the microwave, his gaze fixed upon the clock ticking down the seconds.

"Of course you can. Weren't you the man who finally caught the old catfish at O'Reilly's Cove?"

He tossed her a look with a smile deep in his eyes.

"The same man who threw the catfish back in the water?"

"He'd been around too long for me to be the one to end his life."

"You're a softie, Nick Blackburn. Gramps couldn't believe after hours sitting in the skiff waiting for a fish to take your bait that you managed to bring in the catfish and then you decide to let him go."

"I know. He lectured me the whole way back to the pier that if I'm going to go fishing I should eat what I catch."

"Maybe fishing isn't for you."

"I enjoyed spending time with Nate."

Jesse cracked several more eggs, added milk, salt and pepper, then whipped the contents of the bowl before pouring it into a skillet. "He had a good time. He's never had a chance to show an adult how to do something. He felt very important, especially when his pupil outfished most people who have been trying for that catfish for years. He's been telling everyone he taught you everything you know."

"Is that why Sean wanted my autograph?"

"Yep, you've become a local hero. How did you manage to keep the fish on the line?"

Nick appeared sheepish. "Don't tell anyone I don't know. I guess you can chalk it up to beginner's luck."

"Mom, Cindy and I have set the tables. Anything else you want us to do?"

Jesse began mixing some more scrambled eggs for the second skillet. "Can you two put the pitchers of orange juice out on each table?"

The beep of the microwave sounded and Nick went to work removing the paper plate and sticking another one inside. "How many people are coming for breakfast?"

"About twenty. If we get too many it becomes confusing when we're trying to put everything together later. A few parishioners will stop by this afternoon, but most of the work is done by the committee." Jesse stirred the eggs in the first skillet. "Beth is the organizer of this event every year and it always goes like clockwork. She's very good at organizing."

Nick glanced at the woman taking a batch of biscuits out of the oven. "She does a lot around here."

"I don't know what we would do without her. She's quite remarkable."

"I could use someone like her at my company."

A seed of jealousy took hold and surprised Jesse. Not but a few weeks before, she had been trying to fix Nick up with Beth and now she didn't want— She had no right to be jealous. Nick deserved someone to love him unconditionally. She'd had that once in her life and knew how important that was. She suspected Nick hadn't.

Jesse untied her white apron and hung it up on a hook by the door. "The last pan of biscuits is in the oven. They should come out in about fifteen minutes. I'm going to greet everyone as they arrive and have them start eating. We have a lot to do today."

Nate rushed into the kitchen with Cindy right behind him. "Can we eat now? I'm starved."

"Me, too."

"Sure. Save us a seat. We'll be through in a few minutes."

The microwave beeped again and Nick handled it as though he cooked all the time. "This is much easier than frying bacon in a pan."

"Not as messy, either. Next I have to teach you something more complicated."

"And threaten Boswell? I can't do that to the man."

"I don't think anyone can threaten Boswell. Have you seen Gramps and Boswell when they run into each other out in the yard?"

"They're like rams squaring off."

"And Susan has gone into hiding, which is so unusual for her."

"Can you blame her? Both of them walk by her house several times a day. I've never seen Boswell like this."

"I've never seen Gramps like this, either." Jesse removed the first skillet of scrambled eggs then the second one. She ladled the contents on a large platter.

Zoey breezed by and whisked the platter from her hand to take to the first round table in the rec hall. Jesse made some more for the second table which would be filling up quickly as people arrived.

Fifteen minutes later Jesse and Nick sat down at the third table with Cindy, Nate, Zoey, Beth, Darcy, Joshua and Reverend Collins. Jesse took Nick's and Nate's hands, then bowed her head as the reverend said the blessing. She noticed Nick followed suit after a few seconds of hesitation. Cindy's amen sounded above all the others and brought Nick's head up, a surprised expression on his face.

Jesse began passing the platters around. As she spooned some scrambled eggs onto her plate, she glanced across the table and saw Darcy pass up most of the food, which was unusual for her friend. Darcy's features were pasty.

"Are you all right, Darcy?" Jesse asked while pouring some orange juice into her glass.

Her friend peered at Joshua for a long moment, then said, "My stomach's upset. That's why I was late."

"If you aren't feeling well, you should go home. We can do it without you." Beth drowned her two biscuits in white gravy.

"I'll be fine in a while." Darcy took a deep breath. "I have an announcement. I'm pregnant and have a touch of morning sickness that usually goes away about ten. Then I'll be ravenous."

"That's great news! Congratulations, you two." Jesse lifted her orange juice glass. "Here's to the happy, soon-to-be parents."

"I've got months and months to go. I'm not due until February."

"This is wonderful. I'll get to plan a baby shower," Zoey said, breaking her bacon into pieces to mix with her eggs. "And I have lots of baby clothes you can use if you have a little girl. Tara is growing so fast she hasn't used half of what she has."

The heavy thickness in Zoey's voice caused the people at the table to grow quiet. Jesse's own throat constricted. Her childhood friend had recently returned to Sweetwater, a widow with three children, one born after her husband disappeared, now presumed dead by the government agency he worked for. At least she had known when Mark had died. She had been able to have some closure at the funeral, but Zoey hadn't.

"Mom, can I have some orange juice?" Nate's voice broke into the silence.

Someone at one of the other tables laughed. Another

person said something about children having bottomless pits when it came to food. Relief flowed around the group. Zoey blinked back tears and smiled, her eyes shimmering.

"This is the reason I came back to Sweetwater. It's nice coming home to people who care." Zoey brushed a lone tear from her cheek and picked up her fork to eat her eggs.

Nick leaned close to Jesse and whispered, "I'm beginning to see why you said you take care of your own. I heard about her husband's plane going down in the Amazon. It must be hard not knowing one hundred percent if he's dead or alive. But she seems to be doing okay because of you all." He indicated the people at the table.

"Remember Darcy mentioning us meeting on Saturdays when we were at Harry's Café? We started the group of ladies because of Tanya and Zoey. They need our support."

"That was the meeting you had last week?"

She nodded. "We solved the problems of the world."

How different would his life had been if he had grown up in a town where the people cared what happened to their neighbors? Nick wondered, taking in each adult sitting at the table. They had been friends a long time, had grown up together. He didn't have that. Work had consumed him and that had left little to no time to form friendships. He hadn't even done a good job with his marriage. He and his wife had been strangers living in the same house. Even his relationship with his daughter was much like that. But he was doing something to change that. He would be the kind of father Cindy deserved.

"Who's cleaning up?" Nick asked when he finished the last of his breakfast.

"Everyone." Jesse rose with her plate and utensils.

Nick looked up at her. "Won't that be a bit crowded in the kitchen?"

"Some will clear and throw away the paper plates and cups, plastic utensils, some will wash and put the dishes in the dishwasher and some will stack the chairs and fold up the tables. Shouldn't take too long."

If he hadn't seen it himself, he would have doubted it could be done so quickly and efficiently. No one barked orders or told anyone what to do. People did what had to be done and the rec hall and kitchen were cleaned up in fifteen minutes. Again he felt as though these people worked as a well-coordinated group who had been together a long time and knew each other well. Jesse made sure he was included, but he still felt as though he were that little boy looking through the toy store window at the electric train set that never appeared under his Christmas tree.

After cleanup, the workers began filing into the sanctuary for the short service. Nick hung back to the last, hesitant to go inside. He didn't belong. The strong urge to escape descended, but his feet wouldn't move toward the outside doors. Sweat broke out on his upper lip. Two sets of doors called to him—one offered the escape in his head he knew he should take, the other offered a place in a town that cared. Torn with indecision, he rubbed his hand across his mouth.

Nick took a step toward the double glass doors that

led to the outside. Then another. He stopped and glanced back at the doors that led into the sanctuary. Jesse stood in the entrance into the sanctuary, waiting for him. Her face shone with a radiance and calm acceptance of whatever he chose for himself. She didn't say a word.

You don't belong in there.

God has forsaken you.

There is nothing you can give to these people but money.

Doubt after doubt inundated him. His gaze riveted to Jesse's. She smiled and held out her hand to him.

What if I gave God a second chance? What if He gave me a second chance?

His heartbeat accelerated. He spun on his heel and covered the distance between them. Taking her hand, he squeezed it, the beat of his heart continuing to pound against his chest.

"Are you all right?"

The concern in Jesse's voice and expression touched him, thawing the ice his emotions were encased in—had been for a long time. Why couldn't he have met her years ago—before Brenda, before life had happened? Now it was too late. "I'm fine. I'm a survivor, Jesse, so nothing gets me down for long."

"That's good. I thought for a minute you were leaving."

He peered into the sanctuary and noticed Reverend Collins was about to start the service, but he wanted to ask Jesse something before he lost his nerve. "How do you do it?"

"Do what?"

"Know what a person needs and supply it."

"I'm not sure there's a big secret involved. We pray a lot. We just know usually what needs to be done."

"Are you telling me God tells you?"

"Yes, our faith in the Lord is part of it. We're attuned to each other's needs."

"So when someone's hurting, you're there for him, helping him pick up the pieces."

"I hope so. That's what friends do for each other."

Not from his experience, he thought, the emptiness in him growing, consuming him, refreezing the wall around his heart.

Despairing, he moved into the sanctuary, his fingers linked with Jesse's. That connection made him feel human, almost a part of the town, the church. He grasped on to the bond she offered, and even as they slid into a pew, he didn't release her hand. For a short time he could pretend he belonged.

He finally let go when Reverend Collins said a prayer, asking God to watch over each person before him, to forgive their sins, and to guide them in the ways of Christ. Nick listened to the words and wondered if it was possible for God to forgive his sins—especially the one of turning away from Him, of denying His power.

"Cindy, you can place your doll next to mine." Jesse gestured toward the center table set up for items to be auctioned off the next day.

The child laid the baby girl down next to Jesse's, her

hand lingering on its brown curly hair. "Can I bid on an item?"

"Sure you can."

"Can I bid on the item I gave?"

Jesse knelt down and clasped Cindy's arms, turning the little girl to look at her. "Just because you donated it, doesn't mean you can't bid on it. How much money do you have saved?"

Cindy tilted her head and tapped her finger against her chin. "I think I've got twelve dollars after giving Daddy some money for Crystal's wheelchair." She paused, thought about it and said, "No, I have ten dollars and fifty cents. I bought an ice-cream cone the other day."

"Do you want to give the baby to the auction? It's your decision because you made it."

Frowning, Cindy continued to tap her finger against her chin, taking another moment to think. "I want to give it to the auction. I want to help feed the hungry children."

Her throat tight, Jesse swallowed hard. "Then we will keep the baby in."

Cindy ran her hand over Jesse's doll, a Victorian lady dressed in white lace, black buttoned-up boots, a hat with feathers and a parasol. "I like your doll, too. Do I have enough money for both of them?"

Remembering how much her doll always went for, Jesse smiled and said, "Don't worry. You concentrate on bidding for your doll." She had just decided what she could get Cindy for her birthday.

"Cindy, come on. I need help putting up the streamers." Standing in the doorway to the rec hall, Nate motioned for Cindy.

The little girl whirled around and rushed toward Nate, her pigtails bouncing as she ran. Jesse watched the two children disappear, remembering the sweet gesture Cindy had made. She wanted more children, Jesse thought, sliding her eyes closed, taking a deep, composing breath that still left her chest constricted.

"She certainly is an adorable child."

Jesse gasped, her eyes snapping open. "Beth Coleman, you aren't allowed to sneak up on someone. I think my heart stopped beating."

Beth laughed. "Then quit daydreaming when you should be working."

"You are a hard taskmaster."

"I've raised three siblings. I've had great experience."

"Isn't next semester Daniel's last one?"

Beth's face brightened. "Yes, and then I can do what *I* want."

"Which is?"

"To travel. See the world."

"You're really thinking of leaving Sweetwater?"

"Not permanently but I do want to see what's out there." She leaned close to Jesse. "That's why I wasn't interested in your little matchmaking attempt with your neighbor."

Zoey joined them. "Matchmaking? Jesse? Mom used to write me about your little dinner parties. When I came back, she warned me never to accept an invitation unless I was looking for a man."

Jesse clasped her chest. "I'm shocked. I have friends over for dinner. That is all."

"Where do you want this, Beth?" Joshua asked, carrying a long table with the help of Clint.

"Right next to this one." Beth pointed to the end of the row of tables. "Hey, Clint, didn't I hear that you had to rescue Tara from one of Jesse's dinner parties?"

Clint set the table on the floor, then approached them, sweat beading his brow. "Sure did. If I hadn't, my woman could have been dating Nick Blackburn as we speak." Clint waved his hand toward Jesse. "At least that was *her* plan."

"Clint, my scheme knocked some sense into you." Jesse planted her hands on her hips. "It took my neighbor's interest to spur you into doing what you wanted to do all along."

The man's face blanched. He wiped the sweat from his brow with the back of his hand. Jesse started to kid him about being married when she noticed that several others in the group were looking beyond her shoulder, their expressions troubled. She peered back and found Nick standing a few feet to her left. She gulped and sent up a silent prayer for help. The angry look on Nick's face stole her breath, her thoughts.

Slowly she turned toward him while everyone fled to the four corners, leaving her alone with the man. "How much did you hear?"

"Enough."

"It isn't what it seems."

"And what does it seem?"

The lethal quiet in his voice should have warned her to run while she had the chance. Instead, she stood her ground and said, "That I set—that I used you—" There was no way to explain what she had done except straight out. "I tried to fix you up with various women in town because I thought Cindy needed a mother." She didn't breathe until she finished the last word, then she took in such a deep one that her head swam. She grasped the table's edge to steady herself.

"So when you were dragging me around town introducing me to all these women, you were really trying to fix me up?"

She nodded, not daring to say another word. The fury in his eyes cut through her.

"Even after I told you I didn't want to get married?"

Another nod.

He took a step toward her. "Why?"

She hadn't thought his voice could get any quieter and she'd still hear him, but it did. And it still held a deadly edge to it. She shuddered. "Because Cindy wants a mother." *And because you're dangerous to my peace of mind.*

"I don't have a say in it? You didn't bother to make sure it was something I wanted? What makes you think you know what is best for me and Cindy?" He snapped his fingers. "Ah, I know the answer to that. It's that ability you have of knowing what a person needs before he even knows it."

Sarcasm drenched his words and stung Jesse. She noticed they were the only ones in the rec room. She backed up against the table, wanting to escape as all the others had. "I only wanted to help."

"Did I ask you for your help?"

She shook her head, the thundering of her heartbeat a roar in her ears.

He thrust his face to within inches of hers. "I will not be controlled. I lived in a marriage where my wife tried to control my every move with her behavior. I will not be trapped into a marriage to someone who wants to mold me into someone I'm not."

Trapped between the table and Nick, Jesse had nowhere to go. She could smell the minty flavor of his toothpaste, the lime scent of his aftershave. She could see every harsh line on his face, the hard gleam in his gaze directed totally at her.

"I was wrong. I knew that after Beth, and I stopped. I'm sorry."

He stepped back, giving her some breathing room. Her apology seemed to take the steam out his anger— at least she thought so until he pivoted and headed for the door, saying, "I've got to get out of here."

The rigid way he held his body spoke volumes. He was still furious at her, and she didn't think he would listen to a second apology. She'd never fixed anyone up without his knowledge so why had she with Nick? Because he stirred feelings in her that she thought had died with Mark. She had acted out of desperation to protect her heart. She couldn't risk getting hurt again so she tried to make him unavailable. The only thing was, he was unavailable...but for a different reason.

* * *

The auctioneer held up Jesse's doll to get the bidding started. She chewed on her thumbnail, every muscle taut with stress. The day had started out a disaster and gone downhill from there. She usually had a great time at the Fourth of July celebration, but Nick kept his distance. Cindy sensed the tension between them and asked a zillion questions which she didn't have an answer for.

"One hundred. Do I have 110?"

Jesse blinked, realizing she'd better bid on her doll before someone else got it. She wanted to give it to Cindy as a birthday present. She waved her hand and the auctioneer saw her bid.

"We've got 110. How about 120, folks? This is a genuine Jesse doll. We all know how much work goes into it."

Nick held up his hand.

"One-twenty. Do I hear 130?"

Jesse pressed her lips together and nodded.

"One-forty?"

"One thousand," Nick said, folding his arms across his chest.

The audience gasped. Jesse glared at Nick, but he kept his gaze trained on the auctioneer. The man turned to her. She shook her head.

"I have one thousand. Once. Twice." The auctioneer paused and scanned the audience in the rec hall. "Sold to Mr. Blackburn for one thousand dollars."

As Beth brought the next item up for bidding, the people around Jesse began to whisper among themselves. Nick strode toward the table where he could pick up the doll and pay for it. Several parishioners stared at her, watching her reaction to his taking her doll. She knew everyone knew about their little fight the day before. Two patches of heat scored her cheeks. The walls seemed to be closing in on her.

She spun around and hurried toward the door. As she escaped, she heard Cindy bid five dollars on her doll. She should stay, but she'd had enough of being the object of people's gossiping. She sought the quiet of the garden and the stone bench in the middle.

Shutting her eyes, she listened to the silence that was occasionally broken by a bird's chirping or a car passing on the road in front. She wanted her life to return to normal. She didn't want Nick angry at her.

She heard footsteps approaching. She opened her eyes and saw Nick come to an abrupt stop when he spied her sitting on the bench. He started to turn to leave.

"Don't go."

He froze, his back to her.

"Did Cindy get her doll?"

Slowly he faced her, a cold expression in his eyes. "Yes."

She sighed. "Oh, good. I wasn't sure if ten dollars would be enough."

"What do you mean ten dollars? I paid another thousand for it."

"Do you think money is the answer to all problems?"

The only sign of his own feelings were in the clenching and unclenching of his hands. "It sure can help, especially when you are hungry and need a place to sleep."

"Throwing money at a problem isn't a lasting solution."

"As I understand the object of the auction is to raise money for your outreach projects. So why are you upset? Is it because I outbid you for your doll?"

She shot to her feet, feeling at a disadvantage looking up at him from the bench. "No, that is not it. Cindy was excited about bidding on her doll. She wanted to win it. You took that away from her."

"She wanted her doll that she made. I got it for her. Simple."

"Life isn't always that simple."

"You've got that right—at least not here in Sweetwater. But in Chicago I know the rules. Cindy and I will be leaving early to return home."

"We are?" Cindy asked, hugging her baby doll to her chest.

Chapter Ten

Nick closed his eyes for a few seconds, then turned toward his daughter. "I think it's time for us to go home."

Cindy's bottom lip quivered. Her teeth dug into it. "But we aren't supposed to leave until the end of July."

"Something's come up."

"What?" She clutched her doll tighter to her.

"I need to get back to work."

"But, Daddy, you promised." Tears welled in the child's eyes.

"I'm sorry, princess."

Jesse heard the desperate ring in Nick's voice and wanted to ease the strain between father and daughter. She took a step toward the child.

"You broke your promise." Cindy whirled around and ran from the garden.

The rigid set to his shoulders sagged forward. He dropped his head for a long moment, and if he believed in the power of prayer, Jesse would have thought he was offering up one to the Lord. The fact that he wasn't saddened her. God could help in times of trouble.

"I can talk with Cindy if you want."

He stiffened. "I should never have left Chicago. I know what to expect there."

"But would that have been the best thing for Cindy? Obviously you thought at one time it would be good for you two to get away to really get to know each other. Has that happened? Have you become closer to Cindy?"

He waved his hand toward the area where his daughter had stood a few minutes before. "I would have said yes five minutes ago. Now I don't know."

"I'm sorry. I can't say it any plainer than that. I was wrong to try to fix you up without your knowledge."

Combing his hand through his dark hair, he released a long breath. "What you did made me realize I don't belong here."

"How?"

"Sweetwater is different from Chicago, and I don't mean small town versus big city. It's more than that."

"We care."

"There are people in Chicago who care." Again he ran his hand through his hair, frustration in every line of his body. "I don't know if I can put it into words." He scanned the area as if looking for a way to escape. "I need to find Cindy."

He disappeared quickly, and Jesse collapsed down on the stone bench, wanting to continue their conversation, to explore what was troubling him. She suspected he felt out of his element, therefore not in complete control. And that bothered him—more than he probably would even admit to himself.

The next morning Nate glanced around, then climbed the ladder to the tree house in the large maple tree in the corner of his yard. He scrambled inside, past the sign that read No Girls Alowed, with a big pink X through it. He remembered the day last week when he'd let Cindy change the sign. She'd been laughing as she made the big pink X with a marker. She wasn't laughing now. She was huddled in the corner with her knees drawn up against her chest and her arms clasped about her legs.

"I got your note." Nate sat cross-legged on the wooden planks in front of Cindy.

"I don't wanna leave. Help me."

Nate hated seeing the tears streaming down Cindy's cheeks. They made him sad. "Maybe your dad would let you stay with us. We have an extra bedroom."

She shook her head. "I want him and Boswell to stay, too."

Tilting his head to the side, Nate pulled on his left ear and thought. "You know I saw a movie once where the little boy ran away to keep his parents from getting a divorce and his dad leaving. You could do that."

Cindy's eyes grew wide. "By myself?"

He rubbed the back of his neck and looked out the big hole that served as a window in the tree house.

"Well…well, I guess I could come with you and protect you."

"You would!"

He nodded.

"When? Daddy is talking about leaving soon—maybe even tomorrow."

Nate shifted, rolling his shoulders. "I guess we could today. Right now. I know a place we can hide."

Cindy unclasped her legs and stretched them out in front of her. "I'm kinda hungry. What will we do about food?"

"Go home and get whatever you think you'll need. I'll get some food and meet you back here in half an hour."

Cindy scooted toward the opening that led to the ladder. "Do you think we'll be gone long?"

"Nah. In the movie when the father and mother searched for the little boy, they realized they didn't want a divorce."

"How long did it take?"

"Half a day. So everything will work out and we'll be home by dark."

Cindy went down the ladder first. "Bring a lot of food. I'm really getting hungry."

Jesse put the finishing touches to a doll that depicted a young Colonial girl. She held it up, pleased at how it had turned out. Her curly dark hair reminded Jesse a lot of Cindy. Where were Nate and Cindy? Nate had run in here a while ago and was gone before she had completed dressing the new doll.

The doorbell rang.

Jesse pushed back her chair and went to answer the front door. Surprised to find Nick standing on her porch, she stepped aside to allow him into her house. He stayed where he was, a scowl emphasizing how displeased he must still be with her.

"May I help you?" she asked, leaning against the door, her hand tightly clasped about the knob.

"Have you seen Cindy?"

"Not lately."

"How about Nate?"

"About half an hour ago. Why?"

"I can't find them." He drew in a deep breath, the hard lines of his face deepening even more. "And Cindy's new dolls are gone as well as Oreo."

"Have you checked the tree house? They were up there earlier."

"Yes. No sign of them."

"I'm sure they're around here some place. Let me see if Gramps knows where they went. Come in."

He hesitated, scanning the area before making his way inside.

Jesse closed the door, aware of the level of tension in the small entry hall skyrocketing. She quickly went in search of her grandfather, feeling the scorch of Nick's gaze on her back as though she had done something to cause the kids to disappear.

Jesse found Gramps in the kitchen, rummaging in the refrigerator for something to eat. "Have you seen Nate or Cindy?"

"Nope. Not lately. Where is the ham you had and the sodas? In fact, there were some grapes here a while ago. Where are they?"

Jesse walked to the refrigerator while Gramps moved to the side to allow her to look inside. "That's strange. They were there after breakfast when I put the food up. I was going to make ham sandwiches for lunch." She checked her watch. "In another hour."

"Well, someone took them. And I suspect that someone is Nate." Gramps stepped in front and began searching for something else to eat. "Did he say anything about going on a hike or a picnic with Cindy?"

Jesse shook her head, then because her grandfather was still peering into the refrigerator said, "No. And if he was, he knows he has to get an okay from me."

"Well, there's quite a bit of food missing. Half a loaf of bread is gone, too."

Jesse spun around and headed back to the entry hall, not happy with what she was beginning to think happened. "Gramps doesn't know where the kids are. Was Cindy still upset about leaving earlier than you'd planned?"

He looked away. "I said something about leaving soon at breakfast. She ran off. That's why I was trying to find her to talk to her."

Her stomach muscles twisted into a huge knot. She had a bad feeling about this. "I think maybe our children have decided to run away."

"Why do you think that?"

"She took her favorite things. Nate took some food.

I bet if I look in his room some of his favorite objects will be gone, too."

"Why would they do that?"

"Because Cindy doesn't want to leave Sweetwater."

"We're just leaving a few weeks earlier than we would have. She knew we were only going to be here for a short time."

"Cindy has found a home here." *Even if you haven't,* Jesse silently added.

"Chicago is our home."

Nick said the sentence with such force that Jesse stepped back. "I'm only stating what I see. I know she was looking forward to celebrating her birthday here. She said something to me about it. She has met some children at church she wanted to invite to a party."

"We can have a party in Chicago."

Jesse was beginning to hate the word *Chicago,* especially when Nick said it. "Does she have a lot of friends there?"

"I—" He raked both hands through his hair. "I don't know. Surely she does."

"You don't know?"

"With the wreck everything has been turned upside down. I've been in and out of the hospital. Nothing has been normal. I'm sure she does from school."

"Did she ever bring any friends home?"

He shook his head. "Not for a long time."

"I know you're mad at me, but that doesn't mean you can't stay until the end of July."

His mouth hardened into a grim line. "Let's just find the children."

"You're afraid, aren't you?"

He closed the distance between them, invading her personal space. "Yes, I'm afraid something might happen to Cindy. I would never forgive myself."

"That's not what I meant."

"I know. But I don't want to get into what you were talking about. My focus is on Cindy."

"Nate knows the area and wouldn't let anything happen to her." She finally moved away from him before she tried to smooth away the frown lines on his face. She was sure the children weren't far—they were just hiding, waiting for them to come after them. "I'll tell Gramps. He can help look as well as Boswell. There are a few places we should start with. Some of Nate's favorite hangouts."

Nick watched Jesse leave the entry hall, his body taut, his breathing shallow. He'd come so close to telling her yes he was afraid. Afraid of the feelings he was experiencing toward her. Afraid of what the town of Sweetwater was doing to him, to his family. Afraid of believing again—of giving control of his life over to God.

He'd fought so hard to maintain some kind of control in his life only to have it snatched away in a blink of his eye. One moment he and Brenda had been on the highway, the next they were heading for a large oak tree. In one second his whole life had changed. He'd almost died, nearly lost the use of his leg. Most of all the years he'd thought he had some control over his life had been wiped away with the wreck.

And now his daughter had run away. He couldn't lose Cindy, too. He hadn't yet made up for all the years he'd been too busy working to be the kind of father she deserved.

Lord, if You're listening, please watch over Cindy and help me to find her safe. I know I haven't prayed in years but Cindy is an innocent. She doesn't deserve something bad happening to her. She's already lost her mother. Please protect her and bring her home safe.

The words of his prayer filled his mind and heart with hope. He would find Cindy and she would be all right.

The sun started its descent toward the line of trees to the west. Sweat drenched Jesse's clothes and cloaked her face. She wiped her brow then her neck and looked toward the sun beginning to set.

"It'll be dark in an hour or so," she said, stopping by a tree and leaning against it while she removed her sneaker to dislodge a pebble.

Nick walked a few paces, then stopped when he saw she had. "And we haven't found the children. We should have by now." His cell phone rang and he answered it. When he flipped it closed, he said, "That was Boswell. Nothing."

Jesse's phone went off not a minute later. "Yes?"

"Sorry, Susan and I haven't found them yet. We'll keep looking around the downtown area. I saw Darcy and Joshua and they are searching the eastern part of the lake as well as Zoey and Beth and some others from church. We'll find them, honey."

When Jesse hung up, she didn't look toward Nick for a long moment while she tried to compose herself. She'd been so sure they would find the children in the first hour of searching. They hadn't and now it had been almost eight hours. A tightness in her chest was expanding to encompass her whole body. She felt as though she would shatter any second.

Finally she peered at Nick. "That was Gramps. They've found nothing, but everyone is still looking. We'll find them before dark."

"What if they are hurt? What if—"

"Nick, don't go there. Please, I can't deal—"

She couldn't finish her sentence. Emotions swelled into her throat, closing it. She tried to draw air into her lungs but couldn't seem to get a decent breath. She grasped the tree to steady herself, but the land tilted and spun before her eyes. Squeezing them shut, she continued to inhale until she had forced some fresh air into her lungs.

Nick wound his arms about her and brought her flat against his chest. The rapid beat of his heart mirrored hers. She clung to him. With a light touch he stroked the length of her back over and over.

"We're going to find them, Jesse. I promise you."

She leaned back to stare up into his face. A smile flirted about the corners of her mouth but she couldn't maintain it. "I think we've traded roles."

His mouth lifted in a grin that instantly vanished. "Your optimistic outlook has finally rubbed off on me. Come on. Let's go back to the house and get some flashlights so we can keep going when it gets dark. I won't stop until we find them."

"Knowing the people of Sweetwater, they won't, either. We'll find them. You're right."

He put his arm around Jesse and started back along the lake toward their houses. "That's one of the appealing things about Sweetwater. You aren't alone."

"I can't believe I'm hearing you say that."

"I can respect certain things, but that doesn't mean it is for me. I'm a loner. Have been most of my life."

"Doesn't mean you have to be *all* your life. I can't imagine not having people around me who care what happens to me. I know if I have a problem I have a lot of people I can go to for help. That's comforting."

"The only person I can depend on is myself."

"How about Boswell?"

Nick frowned. "Boswell is an employee. I have good employees who do their job well."

"So if you stopped paying Boswell, he wouldn't care about you or Cindy?"

He was silent for a long moment. "That's a question for Boswell."

"You're ducking the question."

"I don't know the answer."

"I've seen you two interact and you're friends as well as employer and employee." Jesse stepped over a log as they neared her property. She saw her house through the trees. "I have some energy bars. We should get something to eat and drink. It may be a long night."

"While we're here, let's check around. No one has in a few hours."

"Good idea," Jesse said as they emerged from the trees on the west side of her house. She glanced toward the tall maple where Nate had his tree house. In the opening she spied Oreo trying to climb down. She grabbed Nick's arm. "Look."

At a jog he headed toward the ladder and scrambled up it with Jesse right behind him. "Cynthia Blackburn!"

"Is Nate there? Are they all right?" Jesse asked, blocked from seeing inside by Nick's large body.

Nate stuck his head out the window. "I'm here, Mom. We're fine."

Those were the sweetest words she could have heard. As she clung to a rung of the ladder, she sent a silent prayer of thanks to the Lord, then said, "Young man, you get down here right now. I have a few words to say to you and I prefer looking you in the eye when I say them." Jesse hopped to the ground, then backed away from the maple so the rest of them could come down.

Nick stood beside her as both children climbed down the ladder, Cindy holding her two dolls while Nate had Oreo. Jesse had a strong urge to hug her son while she yelled at him. Relief and anger mingled to form a ball of conflicting emotions inside her.

"What do you two have to say for yourselves?" Nick asked, such a quietness to his words that the children's eyes grew round.

Cindy sidled up to Nate and clutched her dolls even tighter. "I don't want to leave early. You promised me."

Her bottom lip stuck out while her eyes glistened with unshed tears.

"Do you two have any idea how much trouble you caused everyone in Sweetwater? Half the town is looking for you." Narrowing her gaze on the pair belonging to her son, Jesse put her hands on her waist.

"They are?" Nate asked, his voice cracking.

"Yes, young man. You have a lot of explaining to do. The first thing you're going to do is write a letter of apology to the people who have given up their time to search for you."

"That's a very good idea, Jesse. Cindy, you can do the same thing."

Cindy and Nate dropped their gazes to the ground, their chins resting on their chests.

"After that you can donate some of your time cleaning up around the church. There are weeds to be pulled, gardens to be tended. I'm sure that Reverend Collins can come up with a list of chores for you to do, Nate."

"Cindy will help him."

"For how long?" Nate brought his head up to look at Jesse.

"I'm so mad at you right now that I'd better not say. I think I might ground you for the rest of your life. So don't push it. Right now you march yourself inside and go straight to your room."

Nate gave Cindy the kitten, then trudged toward the back door. When he reached the deck, Boswell appeared between the two houses. His face lit when he saw Cindy.

"Daddy, are you mad at me?"

"I can't believe you would pull something like running away. I was so worried about you. What if you had gotten hurt?"

"Nate was with me."

Boswell stopped at Nick's side. "Everything okay? Where were they?"

His normal composure was gone. His clothes were dirty and wrinkled as though he had traveled over rough terrain searching for the children. Jesse had never seen Boswell like that. "They were in the tree house."

"But didn't you look there?"

"Yes, but not for a few hours."

"I'm tired. I want to go home." Cindy tried holding both her kitten and dolls, but Oreo slipped from her grasp and darted across the yard. She started after her pet.

"I'll take care of her, sir. You'd better let the authorities and everyone know you've found the children." Boswell hurried after Cindy and the kitten, rounding them up and taking them into the house next door.

With both children safe and inside their homes, Jesse turned to Nick, suddenly aware they were alone. She stared into the liquid darkness of his eyes and remembered how he had held her when she had started to fall apart. If she wasn't careful, she could become used to his particular brand of comfort.

"I don't know how to—" Her cell phone blared, interrupting her thankfully because she wasn't sure what to say to Nick. Instead, she answered her call.

"Just checking in. Find them yet?"

Gramps's gruff question pulled her back to the situation at hand. "Yes, Nick and I did a few minutes ago. They were in the tree house out back."

"But you looked there."

"I think because it was getting dark they decided to come closer to home."

"Have you called the police yet?"

"No. I haven't had time."

"I'll take care of it. I'll also let everyone else know. Then I'm coming home to have a few words with that great-grandson of mine."

When she finished talking with her grandfather, she said, "Gramps will take care of letting people know we found them."

Nick smiled. "I wonder what Boswell thinks of Susan and Gramps together."

"Do you think Boswell really liked Susan?"

Nick lifted his shoulders in a shrug. "It's hard to tell. Boswell is a very private person."

"Like his employer?"

"Yes." Nick's gaze caught hers and held it for a long moment.

A light breeze stirred the summer heat about Jesse. She brushed the damp tendrils away from her face and drew in a deep breath of the rose-scented air. The glittering blue of the lake drew her attention. Its smooth surface reflected the colors of the setting sun—red, orange, pink. Vibrant colors. Ones that reminded a person she was alive, that her son was safe, that the man she had come to care about was only a foot away. She could reach out and grasp his hand, hold on to it and possibly convince him not to leave.

She could. She wouldn't. As the hours had passed and they hadn't found the children, all the pain of losing Mark had come back to haunt her. She had to protect her heart. She couldn't go through losing someone close to her again. It was bad enough that Gramps was getting older and his health was declining.

"We'll stay until the end of July."

Nick's proclamation both frightened and thrilled her. She wanted Cindy—and him—to stay, and yet the more she was around them, the more she wished they were living in Sweetwater permanently. He had made that very clear that wasn't possible. Only heartache laid ahead if she fell in love with Nick Blackburn.

"But I don't want to tell Cindy right away."

"Aren't you risking her doing something like today again?"

"No, because I'm going to make it very clear if she doesn't behave we are leaving immediately. That I will pack up and be gone in an hour's time."

The idea of how quick his presence could be erased from her life gripped her as though a vise held her tight. "I would like to throw her a birthday party. Is that all right?"

"No."

With her emotions swirling in all different directions, Jesse suddenly felt deflated and tried not to show her disappointment. "Why not?"

"Because I am. But I'll accept your help. How about it?" he asked with a smile.

"You've got yourself a partner."

His eyes widened for a few seconds before he said, "Great. I'll have to depend on you to invite all the friends she has made."

"You'd better be careful. Depending on someone? Tsk. Tsk. What will people think?"

"That I have good taste. Who better than you—the woman who knows everyone in town—to tell me whom to invite to my daughter's birthday party?"

Jesse began walking toward her deck. "I'm going to take that as a compliment."

"It was a compliment. I probably know maybe three of the other people who live in my building and that's from seeing them in the lobby."

"Not the elevator?"

"I have a private elevator that goes only to my floor."

"So you don't have to mingle with your neighbors."

"Truthfully, even if I had neighbors next door, I wouldn't have had the time to get to know them. I was always working."

"How are you surviving not working so much?"

He smiled. "At first I thought I would go crazy. Lately I have had a lot of things to keep me occupied."

"Like today."

"That and picnics, fishing trips, dinners."

"So it is possible for you to find things to do besides work and you don't fall apart."

Chuckling, he said, "I would rather not spend another day like this one."

"I agree. I'm exhausted both mentally and physically. After I have a little talk with Nate, I'm heading to bed."

"Without dinner?"

"I don't even have the energy to fix myself something to eat."

He arched a brow. "You've got it bad."

"There you two are," Gramps called out as he and Susan came out of the house and stood on the deck.

"I'll see you tomorrow and we'll coordinate the chores the kids need to do." Nick took her hand and squeezed it before strolling toward his house.

Jesse stared at him for a few seconds, then mounted the stairs to the deck. She noticed her grandfather's arm around Susan's shoulder. The older woman had a huge smile on her face that took years off her age. Her blue eyes twinkled as she edged even closer to Gramps.

"Does everyone know the children are safe?"

"Yes, so you don't have to worry about that. Why did they run away?"

"Because Cindy didn't want to leave and Nate wanted to help her."

"That's my boy, coming to a female's rescue."

"Gramps, I would hardly call what Nate did rescuing Cindy. She wasn't in jeopardy."

"It's all in how you look at it. Just think if Cindy had gone off by herself what kind of trouble the child might have gotten herself in."

Jesse shuddered at the thought. "So you think I should reward my son?"

Gramps shook his head. "Just remember this day could have ended a lot worse. Besides, if Nate and Cindy hadn't run away, I might not be holding Susan right now."

"Gerard," Susan said, playfully punching him in the arm while her cheeks flamed red.

"You know I'm right. You've been avoiding me, but you couldn't ignore a plea to help look for the children."

Jesse narrowed her eyes. "If I didn't know better, I'd think you put the children up to running away."

Susan pulled away. "Gerard, you didn't?"

"No, I would never do that to Nick and Jesse." He grinned. "I was banking on charming my way back into your life. I wasn't going to let an Englishman break us up."

"Us as in a couple?"

Gramps turned fully to face Susan and cupped her face. "Us as in a couple. I love you, Susan Reed, and I want to marry you."

Susan's eyes brimmed with tears. One fell on Gramps's hand. He pulled her against him. "Will you, Susan?"

"Yes. Yes, I will, Gerard Daniels."

Jesse backed away from the pair, wanting to give them some private time. But her heart expanded in her chest, her breath caught in her throat. Her own tears of happiness welled to the surface. What a beautiful way to end a horrible day.

Chapter Eleven

"Is this a weed?" Cindy asked, kneeling in the grass with a bucket half full next to her.

Nate stared at the green plant. "I think anything taller than the grass is a weed."

Cindy yanked on the plant, leaving most of the roots in the ground. She tossed it into the bucket. "When is your mom coming back?"

"She had something to do in the church, then she's going to bring us some sodas to drink."

Cindy dragged the back of her hand across her forehead. "It sure is hot."

"Yep. Let's work over by that tree where it's shady." Nate gestured toward a tall oak.

"Good idea." Cindy hopped to her feet and carried her bucket to a spot under the tree. "I wish I wasn't leaving at the end of next week. Why can't we live here?"

Nate put his bucket next to hers. "You know if my

mom and your dad got married, you could live here in our house. Then you wouldn't have to worry about leaving."

Cindy's eyes brightened. "Yes! That's it. I would love to have Jesse as my mom."

"And your dad is cool."

Cindy's bright expression dimmed. "But how do we get them together?"

"I saw a movie once where two girls got their mom and dad alone on a date and everything worked out."

"Yeah, that could work. We're usually around when they're together." Cindy thought for a moment. "But how are we gonna do that?"

Grinning, Nate explained, "We'll plan a picnic at O'Reilly's Cove and not show up."

"I thought Gramps and the kids were going to be here. Where are they?" Jesse looked around O'Reilly's Cove and only saw a sandy beach and a large rock slide jutting out into the calm blue water. No skiff. No people other than she and Nick.

"Look." He pointed toward a picnic basket with a blanket spread out under an elm tree. "They must be around here somewhere. They've left the food. I'm hungry. Let's see what they fixed for lunch."

On top of the basket there was a note weighted down with a rock keeping it from blowing away. Jesse recognized her grandfather's handwriting and picked it up and read it aloud. "'Enjoy. Decided to take the kids with me to look for a ring for Susan. We'll be back when we are through.'" She crunched the paper into a ball. "I thought I was going with Gramps to help with the ring."

"I can't believe the kids agreed to go—" Nick rubbed his chin. "Unless they're up to something."

"What?"

"Take a look around. Secluded cove. Basket full of food. A blanket. What does that bring to mind?"

"A date?"

Nick nodded.

"You know, I've heard those two whispering a lot lately. Yesterday at church when I brought them their sodas while they were weeding, they were giggling and giving me strange looks. I should have figured they were up to something. We should just leave and meet them in town—if they are really going to look for a ring, that is."

"And give up all this food? Let's eat first, then surprise them at the jewelry store."

"I guess. I am hungry." Jesse lifted the lid on the basket. She began laying out the cartons of food.

"I can tell Boswell wasn't in on their scheme. This all looks like it came from a fast-food chicken place."

"This no doubt is Gramps's contribution to the plan. He thinks all food should be fried, even vegetables."

Sitting on the blanket near Jesse, Nick took a piece of fried chicken and bit into it. "Not bad."

"Mine's better. I have a secret batter recipe that was passed down in my family." Jesse went straight to the coleslaw, loving this particular place's recipe. "Do you want any of this?" she asked in a generous mood as she held up the container.

"Nah. I think I'll stuff myself on chicken. I don't get fried food often. Boswell's on a health kick."

"Since you're a meat-and-potato kind of guy, I'll let you have the mashed potatoes while I eat the biscuits." She bent closer to whisper, "But don't tell anyone that our lunch isn't what you would call well balanced."

He inhaled a deep breath. "You smell good."

His smile curved his full mouth and centered her attention on it. For a second she allowed herself to respond to his compliment, a warmth flowing through her. Then her panic took hold and she said, "That's because we didn't walk here but drove instead." She leaned away, reminding herself not to get too close to Nick. That was when she started thinking things that weren't possible.

His chuckle mingled with the sounds of water lapping against the shore, a bird up in the elm tree above them, the rustle of the leaves from the gentle breeze. "True."

The warm feeling returned and chased away the panic. She raised her gaze to his, the mischievous gleam pulling her even closer to him. His mouth that looked so good with a smile on it was a whisper away from hers. So much for putting distance between them, she thought, her eyes sliding closed.

His thumb touched her lips first, caressing her with a lightness that shivered down her. Then his mouth claimed hers and she could taste the spicy chicken he'd been eating as well as the mint of his toothpaste. Those sensations heightened the intimacy of the moment as his arms went about her and drew her against him.

The sound of a flock of geese flying overhead broke them apart. Jesse scooted away, needing to put that space between them before her emotions were totally involved. Who was she kidding? They were totally involved and she was going to end up getting hurt. More than ever she needed to back off.

She propped herself up against the tree trunk and ate her coleslaw while Nick silently finished off two more pieces of chicken, then started in on the mashed potatoes. A frown descended over his features the longer he sat across from her as though he didn't like the direction his thoughts were going in.

"When you go back to Chicago, what are you going to do?"

He continued eating, his gaze trained on a spot between them. "Work. That's all I know how to do. I've neglected my company long enough."

"How about Cindy?" Her original assessment that the child needed a mother hadn't changed.

"I'll adjust my schedule to accommodate Cindy."

"Are you listening to yourself? You make her sound like she's part of your work to be squeezed in accordingly."

His head jerked up and his regard sharpened, cutting through her. "Cindy will be my number one priority."

"She isn't a job. She's your daughter."

This time he surged to his feet. "I know she's my daughter. I don't need you to tell me that. Nor do I need you to tell me how to raise her."

"She told me she wants to take dance lessons. Did you know that?" Jesse rose, squaring off in front of

Nick, ready to do battle for the little girl she had come to love like her own.

"No."

"She wants to get to know a girl on the third floor in your building, invite her over to play. She wants you to read bedtime stories to her like you are now. She wants to go to her mother's grave site and put flowers on it. You haven't taken her and she doesn't understand why."

With each sentence Nick winced until pain crumbled his defenses and shone through. "Because I can't bring myself to go to Brenda's grave. She nearly killed me and sometimes I think it was intentional. I think she was willing to die as long as she could take me with her."

Jesse sucked in a breath and held it until her lungs burned. She didn't know what to say to that assertion. She blinked, trying to assimilate what he had told her about his deceased wife. "I thought it was an accident."

"That's what the police report says, but you didn't see her face right before we went off the road and toward the tree. It was full of hatred, all directed at me." He shuddered, hugging his arms to his chest as if to ward off a chill even though the temperature was over ninety degrees.

"I'm sorry." She wanted to go to him but something in his stance forbade it.

"Do you know what my first coherent thought was when I woke up in the hospital?"

She shook her head, her heart bleeding for him.

"I was glad she was dead," he said, his voice weak, his breath ragged, his expression full of self-hatred. "I wished for someone to be dead. How can your God forgive that?"

"He can be your God, too. You can start by asking Him for forgiveness and then forgiving yourself."

"I didn't think I could hate someone so much, but Brenda made my life at home unbearable to the point I never wanted to be there. So I did what I had been doing for years. I worked fourteen-, fifteen-hour days. I missed the first six years of Cindy's life. I'm just beginning to really know my daughter."

She couldn't stay away from him another second. Jesse took him into her embrace and held him tight against her. She felt him shudder again and again as though he were reliving the wreck and his feelings all over. "Turn to the Lord. If you truly want forgiveness, He will. But you should also forgive Brenda. Until you do, you won't be totally free of the past. It will always be there to drag you down."

When Nick backed away, he scanned the area, his composure falling into place as though he hadn't opened up to her and let her glimpse the pain he felt. "I've had enough of communing with nature. Let's go find the children."

"It shouldn't be too hard to find Gramps's old truck in town," she said, picking up on his need to lighten the mood. "I have a couple of ideas where they might be."

"Not the jewelry store?"

"I doubt it. If they went, Gramps wouldn't stay long. He'd pick the first ring he saw that he could afford. Gramps and shopping do not go together."

Nick helped Jesse put the food into the basket, then

he folded the blanket and they headed for his SUV. The drive into town was done in silence. Jesse watched out the side window. The lake and woods disappeared as Nick turned onto the road that led to the downtown area of Sweetwater. She said nothing further about the torment eating at Nick, but it was there between them, making the quiet tension-packed.

On Main Street Jesse straightened and pointed toward Gramps's old red pickup. "Just as I suspected. They're at Harry's, probably having lunch."

"If I know Cindy, she's having more than lunch. She has developed a fondness for Harry's vanilla milkshakes." Nick parked two doors down from the front of the café. "I'm glad it's past lunchtime or we'd never have gotten a parking spot so close."

Coming around the front of his car, Jesse shaded her eyes and studied Nick for a moment. "You're getting to know Sweetwater quite well. Be careful or someone might mistake you for a native."

"Never. I have *big city* written all over me."

She gestured at him. "Take another look at yourself. Jean shorts, T-shirt and tennis shoes. You don't appear very big city to me."

He frowned at her as he opened the door to Harry's.

Jesse spotted the children and Gramps at the back in a booth. The waitress was clearing off the table, leaving only the milkshakes that each one of them had ordered as a dessert.

Cindy sucked on her straw so hard her cheeks went in. "Daddy," she said when she saw him negotiating his way toward the booth. "You weren't on your picnic very long."

"We were dying to see what ring you all picked out." Nick slid in next to Cindy and Nate.

Jesse took the seat across from Nick next to Gramps. "Yeah, where is it?"

Her grandfather stirred his chocolate milkshake with his straw, seemingly fascinated by the swirling motion he had created.

"Gramps, the ring."

He looked up. "We haven't gone yet. We all decided we needed nourishment before making the big decision so we stopped in here first."

Jesse propped her folded arms on the table. "That's great! Then Nick and I can give our two cents' worth."

Gramps scowled. "Don't need a whole army going into the small jewelry store. You two go find something else to do."

She leaned toward his ear and whispered, "You're not being very subtle."

"I'm never subtle. You're a young, attractive woman who should be dating instead of trying to fix every Tom, Dick and Harry up with a date."

"Who's Tom?" Cindy asked.

"And Dick?" Nate asked, then turned to Cindy and added, "Harry must be the owner of the café. But I thought he was married to Rose."

"Figure of speech, kids." Gramps waved his hand over the table. "Your mother is concerned about every-body else's love life but her own."

Red-hot flames had to be licking at her face because Jesse felt on fire. "Gramps!"

"Well, it's the truth, young lady. You have so much to offer a man. You know how to cook and keep a house. You're a terrific mother and you were a great wife to Mark."

Jesse rose on shaky legs, gripping the edge of the table to keep herself upright. She wanted to throttle her grandfather. She'd never been so embarrassed in her whole life. "I need some fresh air." She spun on her heel and fled the café, aware of the stares from the other patrons.

She heard Nick say something to the group then him following her. Her feet couldn't carry her fast enough—away from her family, away from Nick. All she wanted to do was hide. Nick clasped her shoulder halfway down Main Street and halted her progress toward the park.

"Hold up. My mending leg can't keep up with you. I'm not up to jogging yet."

He could have said a lot of things that wouldn't have stopped her, but that did. She glanced back at him, seeing the grimace around his mouth that indicated he had overused his leg. "Sorry about that."

"You know, your grandfather has a point. One of the things I like about you is your caring and concern for others."

His words cooled the heat of embarrassment blanketing her face. She turned completely around. "Are you still angry with me for trying to fix you up without your knowledge?"

"I have discovered fixing people up is part of who you

are. I do recommend in the future making sure all parties are aware of what you're doing." Linking his hand with hers, he started walking toward the park. "I am curious why you haven't tried your skills on yourself."

"I've been married. As I've told you before, I'm not interested in getting married again. It's someone else's turn at happiness." Even to Jesse's own ears her words lacked her usual conviction.

"I've been married, too. That didn't stop you from trying with me."

"But you weren't happy, and besides, Cindy wants a mother."

"And Nate doesn't want a father?"

His question brought a halt to her step. She'd known Nate needed a man's influence and had hoped that Gramps would be it. She loved her grandfather, but Nate needed more than Gramps could give him. "I've never asked him."

"You have a wonderful child who would make any man proud to call son."

"I know."

"Then what's the problem?"

I'm the problem, she thought. *How can I risk that kind of hurt again? How do I deserve happiness when—* She shrugged as though she didn't have an answer.

"You've never been tempted with all those men you've fixed up?"

"Never once." *Until you,* she added silently.

"That's hard for me to believe with all your warmth and kindness."

"Well, it's true. It's easier not to get involved."

He moved in front of her and blocked her path. "Why? I know why I say that. But your marriage was a good one. Why wouldn't you want to experience that again?"

"I've had my chance."

"Where's it written down that everyone only gets one chance at a happy marriage?"

"I didn't say that."

"You've implied it. Didn't you tell me Darcy had a good marriage the first time around and now the second time, too?"

She chewed on her bottom lip, trying to figure out how to stop the direction the conversation was going. "We need to discuss Cindy's party. What can I do to help?"

"You aren't going to get out of discussing this by asking a question. I may not be as good a listener as you are, but something isn't right here. You're avoiding my questions, giving partial answers, not the complete truth. Why?"

She moved around him and headed for a wooden bench by the fountain in the center of the park. Again she heard him right behind her, not allowing her to get away. When she sat, he eased down next to her, his thigh touching hers, his presence trapping her.

"I'm not going anywhere. What's troubling you?"

"Is this how you made your millions? Dog someone until they do what you want?"

"Yep. That particular skill has come in handy on a number of occasions and you aren't going to change the subject."

She stared at the cars that passed the park on Main Street. She would never forget the evening her husband had died. The memory trembled through her with such a force she shook. Folding her arms to her, she said, "You might not think so highly of me if you knew the truth."

"What truth?" he asked in such a low voice that it barely sounded.

"I'm the reason my husband is dead. Not quite the paragon of virtue, am I?"

"Why don't you tell me what happened?"

Again that quiet voice that forced her to listen carefully to him. Her teeth dug into her lip, the words stuck in her throat. She hadn't shared her private, innermost thoughts on her husband's death with anyone.

He took her hand and laced his fingers through hers.

She peered at their hands linked together and said, "I had taken his hammer outside to fix some outdoor furniture we had in the yard. It started to rain and he didn't want it left out there. He was very particular about his tools. When he ran out to get the hammer, lightning struck him."

"So you blame yourself for his death because you left the hammer outside in the rain? Do I have it right?"

She nodded, her throat clogged with emotions long buried.

"It was a freak accident. He didn't have to go get it. He chose to. Remember, free will."

"But I knew how he was about his tools. He was especially particular about that hammer because it had been his dad's. I shouldn't have used it. Or at the very least, I should have put it back when I was through."

"Why didn't you?"

"Nate fell and hurt his knee. I took him inside to clean him up and then forgot about the hammer until it started to rain."

"Why did your husband go out and not you?" He shifted on the bench so he could face her.

"Because I have always been afraid of thunderstorms and he knew that. He went because he knew how upset I was getting. The weather was starting to get bad."

"It wasn't your fault. None of it. You can't keep beating yourself up over an accident, an act of nature."

"One minute Mark was here, the next he was gone. I can't go through that again. It hurt too much."

Nick slipped his arm about her shoulder and pulled her against him. "I'm finding out the hard way we can't control our lives like we wish we could."

"But if I had just—"

He laid his finger over her mouth to still her words. "Weren't you the one who told me I had to forgive myself if I wanted to move on with my life? You need to practice what you preach."

"I'm trying."

"Do you think God blames you for Mark's death? Or does anyone else?"

"No."

"Then you need to quit blaming yourself. We can't completely control life. I am slowly discovering that truth. I've tried for years and haven't really succeeded.

We are quite a pair. Full of guilt," he said with a laugh that held no humor.

"So what are we going to do about it?"

"Half the battle is knowing what the problem is." He rose and extended his hand. "Let's go back and get a milkshake. I happen to share a fondness for one, like my daughter has."

Jesse placed her hand in his. Was she using her guilt over Mark's death to keep her rooted in the past? The past was a known entity—the future wasn't.

Chapter Twelve

Nate pushed Cindy higher in the swing on the church playground. "Let me know if you want me to stop."

She giggled, the wind blowing her long hair behind her and cooling her face. "I love to swing and try to see over the trees."

"Me, too."

When Cindy finally came to a stop and got off to let Nate use the swing, she said, "We're leaving the day after my birthday party."

"That's in three days." Nate plopped down on the wooden seat and gripped the ropes.

Cindy positioned herself behind him and gave him a push. "Do you have any more ideas? I don't want to leave." She belonged in Sweetwater. Why couldn't her daddy see that? She had friends and her daddy laughed now. He never had before.

"I don't know what else to do. We've tried to leave

our parents alone, but it hasn't done anything. Why don't you tell your father you want to stay? He might decide to. He came to church today when you asked him to."

"Maybe…if I tell him how bad I want it." She pushed Nate again. "Then if we stay, he can marry your mom." *That's a perfect plan,* Cindy thought and smiled.

Nick wandered along the path in the garden beside the church, drawn to the pond with goldfish and a small waterfall, its sound soothing to the soul. Was he using his anger like a shield to keep himself isolated from people? He couldn't deny that for a good part of his life, his anger toward the Lord had consumed him. And look where it had led him—alone, struggling to get to know his daughter.

He sat on the large rock beside the pond and stared at the clear water with orange goldfish swimming about the green plants. But where did he go now? He needed to get back to something familiar. He felt so lost. Too many things had changed in his life lately.

Lord, show me the way. What should I do?

The plea came from his heart, battered and bruised. The minute evolved into ten and still nothing stood out as a clear path for him to follow. He rose, berating himself for thinking an answer would come just because he'd finally asked. He shook his head, turning from the pond. He wasn't good at asking for help. He started back toward the church parking lot to find Cindy and leave.

His daughter stood next to Jesse and Nate. When she saw him, she ran toward him, a huge grin on her face. She skidded to a stop and began to pull him toward Jesse.

"We're invited to another fish fry tonight. Gramps caught a whole bunch yesterday."

Gramps? When had his daughter begun calling Gerard Daniels Gramps? Alarm bells rang in his mind. The feeling of being trapped closed in on him.

"Honey, we have a lot to do in the next few days before we leave. Don't you—"

Cindy stopped, a pout replacing her grin. "I want to live in Sweetwater, Daddy, all the time. I don't want to leave in a few days. I hate Chicago."

He stooped in front of her and clasped her arms. His leg ached from pushing himself too much that morning when he'd exercised, but he needed to make it clear to Cindy their home was in Chicago. "Hon, we have to leave. My work is there. Maybe we'll come back for a holiday next summer."

"You run the company. Why can't you run it here? You have been."

He hadn't allowed himself to think of that possibility because it opened up too many unknowns. He already had little control over his life. How could he give up all of it? Sweetwater was a nice place to visit. But to live here? He slowly rose, the pain in his leg sharpening. He focused on it, pulling his thoughts away from the prospects of settling down in a small town.

Jesse waved him to her. "Did Cindy ask you about

the fish fry? Gramps got some tasty catfish. You know, that secret batter I use for chicken I also use for catfish."

The urge to say no was strong, but one look at Cindy's eager expression and he found himself saying, "Sure. Can I bring anything?"

"Nope. I've got things covered. Boswell's welcome to come, too."

"Are Gramps and Susan going to be there?"

"Yes. Gramps is giving her a ring this afternoon when he picks her up so she'll be showing it off."

"Do you think it's wise then to have Boswell there?"

"We can't leave him out of our family plans." The second Jesse said *our family* her eyes widened and her mouth snapped close. She swallowed hard. "I mean, Gramps will be fine. He and Susan are engaged."

Nick took Cindy's hand, needing some space. Suddenly his chest felt tight, and it was difficult to draw in a good decent breath. "I'll ask Boswell. What time?" He stepped back.

"Six. Nate wants to play croquet after dinner. Up for a game?"

"Sure." Nick backed away some more, pulling Cindy with him. "See you then." He turned and started for his SUV.

"But, Daddy, I wanted to stay and—"

"I need to get home and make some calls. You can see Nate later."

He would call his top executives and set a meeting for first thing Friday morning. Then he wouldn't be tempted to stay another weekend that might evolve into more.

* * *

Jesse stared out the window over the sink toward Nick's house. "Cindy, you did say your father would be coming shortly?"

"Yes, he's been on the phone most of the afternoon, but he told me he would be along soon." The little girl stirred the secret batter.

"Where's Nate?"

"Getting the croquet set out."

"If you want to help him, I can finish dinner by myself."

Cindy hopped down from the stool. "Okay. But I want to help fry the fish. Will you call me when you need me?"

"Yeah." Jesse put the batter mixture into the refrigerator to keep until she cooked the fish.

When the little girl left, Jesse checked the stove clock. Six-thirty. It wasn't like Nick to be late. She heard the front door open and close and Gramps call out to her.

"I'm in here."

Gramps and Susan came into the kitchen. Jesse dried her hands on her apron as she moved toward the couple.

"Let me see the ring."

Susan displayed the half carat, emerald-cut diamond in a gold setting.

"It looks wonderful on your hand. Welcome to the family, Susan." Jesse hugged the older woman, a sudden well of tears filling her eyes. She was so glad Gramps had found someone after being a widower for twenty years.

"Who else is coming to dinner? Is this one of your little dinner parties to fix someone up?" Susan asked, splaying her fingers to look at her own engagement ring as though she didn't believe it was on her hand.

"I'm retiring."

"Why?" Gramps asked, walking to the stove to check what was cooking. He lifted a lid and took a deep breath. "I love green beans and new potatoes. And, Susan, this is why I go fishing so much. For the fish Jesse fries up for us."

"I'm through meddling in other people's lives," Jesse finally answered her grandfather as he finished peeking into the pots on the stove.

"You weren't meddling. You were trying to help." Gramps put his arm around Susan's shoulder. "If I'm not mistaken, you fixed us up."

"I was meddling." Jesse went back to the counter, as surprised as Gramps and Susan at her declaration. She hadn't thought about the decision; it had just come out. Now that she thought about it, however, it was for the best. "Look what almost happened with you two. You and Boswell almost got into a physical fight."

"But that wasn't your doing. That was me. I set out to make Gerard jealous and it worked a little too well."

"You did!" Gramps stared at Susan.

"Yes. If I hadn't, you might have continued to be content with just dating. I wanted something more."

Gramps beamed. "You never said anything."

"I'm so glad everything worked out for you two."

Jesse walked to the stove to turn down the temperature on the food since Nick hadn't arrived yet.

"How about you and a certain young man?" Susan snuggled closer to Gramps.

"By the way, where is Nick?"

"I don't know. He hasn't come yet." Jesse latched on to her grandfather's question, hoping that Susan wouldn't pursue hers.

"You two sure have been seeing a lot of each other. Anything you want to tell us?"

Jesse should have known that Susan wouldn't let the topic go. She was the town gossip, after all. "He's a good friend."

"There's something to say about being good friends. Sometimes it leads to a relationship beyond friendship," Susan said.

"Not in this case. He's leaving on Thursday."

"Someone should shake some sense into you two," Gramps said, starting for the back door. "Are Nate and Cindy outside?"

"Yes," Jesse said as her grandfather and Susan went in search of the children, leaving her alone with her thoughts.

She went back to the sink and looked out the window toward Nick's house. What if he decided to stay in Sweetwater? What would she do? She thought about him being her permanent neighbor and a warm glow suffused her. Something beyond friendship? Was that possible considering their problems? A picture of two households blending into one began to take root in her mind until she put a halt to the dream. That was all it was. A dream. Something just out of reach.

A movement out the window caught her attention. Nick strode toward her backyard. Her heart increased its beating as she anticipated him knocking on the kitchen door. When the sound came, she hurried to answer it.

The first thing she noticed when she opened the door were the tired lines about his eyes. She stepped to the side to allow him to enter, shoving the dream to the dark recesses of her mind.

"Is everything okay?"

He kneaded the cords of his neck. "Yeah. Just had some business to take care of. So much to do when I return to Chicago."

The image of them as a couple vanished completely at those words. At every turn possible he made it clear he was going back to Chicago after Cindy's birthday. "I thought your company was running smoothly."

"It is. I have a good staff, but still I have let things slide this past year. I'm thinking of expanding into a different market. I want to get moving on those plans once I return."

It didn't appear as though this past year had really changed anything with Nick. His life would continue to revolve around his work with his family—Cindy—coming in second place. Her heart twisted with that thought.

"Where does Cindy fit into your plans?"

"I won't neglect her."

"What about attending church? She has shown such an interest in God and Jesus."

"If she wants to continue attending, I can take her."

"I'm glad." Some of her worries eased as she headed back to the stove to finish preparing the fish to fry.

"I saw Susan and Gerard on the deck. Susan is sporting quite a rock."

So now they had progressed—or rather regressed—to small talk. "Yeah. I'm so happy for them. Where's Boswell? Isn't he coming?"

"He'll be along in a little while. He was packing some boxes for the move and wanted to finish what he'd started."

Again a reference to his leaving. Jesse sighed, trying to keep a rein on her emotions, at least glad that he was open to going to church with Cindy. But she hadn't thought she would be so affected by her neighbor's departure. She had come to care about Cindy—and Nick. She would miss them, and so would Nate.

"Can I help you with anything?" Nick asked, standing in the middle of her kitchen, surprisingly looking at home there.

She removed the bowl of batter for the fish from the refrigerator. "Cindy wanted to help me fry these. Can you tell her I'm ready?"

"Sure. Anything else?"

"Nope. That should about do it. We'll eat in about twenty or thirty minutes."

When Nick left, Jesse sagged against the counter, drained emotionally. This was a celebration of Gramps and Susan's engagement, but for the life of her she didn't feel like celebrating. Sadness encased her in a cold blanket.

* * *

"I'll get it," Cindy yelled when the doorbell rang.

She ran to it and tugged the door open. Nate stood on the porch with a red-orange-and-yellow wrapped present in his hands.

"Come in." Cindy grabbed his arm and dragged him inside. "You're the first to arrive. I need to talk to you."

"What's wrong?"

"Everything." She placed the present on the table in the entry hall, pulled him toward the den and shut the door. "We're going for sure. I've tried talking to Daddy, but no matter what I say he isn't changing his mind. My things are packed. What do I do now?" The question ended on a sob.

"I don't know. Let me think." Nate paced about the room, his features pinched into a frown. Suddenly he stopped and faced Cindy. "I've got it. Whenever Mom has a problem, she prays about it. She tells me it always helps. Why don't you pray about staying in Sweetwater?"

"Yes. God will listen." Cindy threw her arms about Nate and hugged him tight. When she pulled away, his cheeks were flaming red. "You are the best friend I ever had." His face grew even redder.

The door to the den opened and Nick stepped inside. "Cindy, you've got friends arriving. You should be greeting them."

"I wanted to say goodbye to Nate." Cindy hurried past her father.

"We're not leaving yet," Nick said, but Cindy was halfway down the hall.

Nate started after Cindy.

"Is Cindy all right?" Nick asked, his words stopping the boy.

"She wants to stay here."

"I know. I wish we could but—" Nick couldn't explain to the child his need to return to his normal life. This time in Sweetwater was a summer holiday, never meant to extend beyond July.

Nate smiled. "Everything will work out. You'll see."

The boy's optimism panicked Nick. "You two aren't planning on running away again, are you?"

"Oh, no. We learned our lesson. Mom was so upset with me, and I don't want to worry her like that again."

Relief slumped Nick's shoulders. "Good. I don't want to worry like that again, either." The sound of children's voices floated to Nick. "We'd better see who has arrived."

Cindy tore into the wrapping paper on the gift that Nate had given her. Inside was a male doll made by Jesse that complemented the one her father had won at the auction. A grin lit the little girl's face. "I love it. Thank you, Nate." She looked toward Jesse. "And you."

"You're welcome. I have another present for you." Jesse moved through the children sitting around Cindy watching her open her gifts.

"You do?"

Jesse handed her the present she had specially picked out for the child.

Cindy took the paper off more carefully this time,

and when she revealed the gift, a look of awe graced her features. "A Bible."

"I thought you should have your own."

"Thank you." Cindy stared at the book for a long moment, her fingers tracing the gold lettering of her name, engraved on the black leather.

"I hope everyone is hungry. The pizzas are here," Boswell announced from the doorway. "We are eating out on the deck."

Ten children hopped to their feet and raced toward the back of the house. The room was emptied in less than a minute except for Nick, Jesse and Cindy.

Cindy rose more slowly and walked to Jesse. The child hugged her. "Your gifts were perfect. I love you."

Jesse smoothed Cindy's hair back from her face. Her throat swelled with emotions. Swallowing several times, she said, "I love you, too. You're a special little girl."

She tugged Jesse down closer so she could whisper in her ear, "I have a plan. The Bible will help me with it." She kissed Jesse on the cheek, then hurried from the room.

Stunned, Jesse straightened, her gaze locked with Nick's equally surprised expression. "It was Cindy's birthday, but I think I got the best gift of all."

Gone was Nick's shock to be replaced with a frown. He stalked past Jesse, leaving her alone in the living room. Nick's reaction to Cindy's statement dashed any hope that he was considering staying in Sweetwater. Why had she clung to the hope that he might have wanted to? She hadn't wanted to get involved with anyone.

Then why does it hurt so much to see his frown?

She wanted to escape to the safety of her home, away from Nick, away from the dream she was beginning to have—Nick, her, Nate and Cindy as a family. But she wouldn't. This was Cindy's special day and she was determined to stay no matter how much her heart was breaking. When they were gone tomorrow, she would put her life back together. She had done it once after Mark's death, and she had known her husband for years. This shouldn't hurt as badly. But it did.

Jesse headed into the kitchen to see if she could help Boswell. He came through the back door with an empty platter. "Need any help?"

"Yes, out there corralling eleven children." He motioned toward the deck with his head.

"Are you sure you don't want me to help get the food ready?"

"There's nothing else to do but take the cake out and dish up the ice cream."

"I can do that."

Boswell stopped reaching for the cartons of ice cream from the freezer and stared at her. "What's the problem?"

"I prefer working behind the scenes."

He studied her for a moment. "Fine. I'll take the cake out. Why don't you put some ice cream in each bowl? I'll be back in a minute to get them."

"Thank you," she said, realizing she sounded almost desperate. She was glad Boswell hadn't commented on her tone of voice.

Jesse busied herself dishing up the chocolate ice

cream into red plastic bowls, then sticking red plastic spoons in each one. She had finished with the last bowl when the back door opened. She spun about with a smile, thinking it was Boswell returning for the ice creams. Instead, it was Nick.

She stiffened, her smile vanishing.

Boswell hurried around Nick and placed the bowls on the large platter, then he was gone. Nick continued to stare at her with a penetrating gaze that caused her muscles to grew tighter.

When Nick finally spoke his tone was low, void of any emotion. "Thank you for getting the clown. The children really enjoyed him, especially the animals he made out of balloons."

"No problem. Ken loves to perform."

"I also appreciate your arranging for the children from the Sunday school class to come to the party. Cindy's having a great time."

Such polite strangers, Jesse thought. Is this what it is going to come down to? To part as though they never knew each other? For close to two months Nick and Cindy had consumed her every thought and awakened moments. How was she supposed to say goodbye tomorrow and not be affected?

Because his gaze had narrowed on her face as though he were trying to read her innermost thoughts, Jesse turned away and cleaned up the mess she had made spooning the ice cream into the bowls. Her hand shook as she wiped the counter. "I'm glad the party is a success."

"Only because of you."

A wealth of emotion sounded in his voice so close that she jumped, startled by his nearness. She whirled about. Nick stood not a foot from her and she hadn't even heard him moving toward her. For a few seconds his vulnerability that he had occasionally allowed her to see flashed into his eyes, making them dark. Automatically she started to reach for him. He saw and backed up, an arm's length away.

"I wish things could have been different between us, Jesse, but I'm no good at marriage. It's best I leave and, frankly, coming next summer wouldn't be a good option for either one of us."

With her heart cracking into pieces, she nodded. "Of course, you're right. Why subject each other to our presence? And Cindy doesn't need false hope. She's been through enough without having her think there could be more between us." She was amazed at how calm her voice was while inside she was coming apart atom by atom.

"It's not you, Jesse. It's me. I did a lousy job with my first marriage. I don't repeat mistakes."

"I see you still haven't forgiven yourself, have you?"

"I'm working on it. I'm learning to pray again." He released a heavy sigh. "My life has been so mixed up this past year. I need to get back to what is familiar. Nothing has been and I feel so lost at times."

Jesse began to gather the pieces of her heart to her; she began to erect a barrier between herself and Nick. She had to if she was going to get through his departure. "I imagine when you get back to Chicago, Sweetwater will seem like a nice but brief interlude in your life. I'm glad you're exploring your relationship with God. He will help you when you need it. Now I'd better get out there before Cindy wonders where I am." She started past him.

He grasped her arm and halted her step. "Jesse, I wish it could—"

"Hey, I enjoyed your company and friendship, but it is time to move on. I told you at the beginning I wasn't looking for anything more than friendship." She didn't tell him that had changed somewhere over the weeks she had gotten to know him. She didn't want him to feel any worse than he already did about leaving Sweetwater.

"Sure." He released his grip on her arm and watched her walk to the door.

The drill of his gaze into her back propelled Jesse to move fast before her facade crumpled and she wept for what wouldn't be…in front of him.

Out on the deck the warm July sun heated her body but didn't completely rid her of the chill that was embedded deep in her bones. She rubbed her hands up and down her arms to chase the cold away. Focusing on the eleven children sitting at the long table eating cake and ice cream, she forced herself to live for the moment— not in the past and certainly not in the future.

But as she approached Cindy, she thought that in twenty-four hours she would be gone from her life— Nick would be gone—for good. She offered the child a false smile while inside a part of her froze.

* * *

Dressed and ready to leave Sweetwater, Cindy knelt by the bed and clasped her hands. "God, I need Your help. I want Daddy to stay here. I want Daddy to marry Jesse. Please help me find a mother."

"Cindy, are you ready to go?" Nick peered around the partially opened door. "What are you doing, princess?"

Cindy rose. "Praying to God about staying here."

Nick felt as though his daughter had reached into his chest and squeezed his heart in her fist. He wished he could give her what she wanted; he just couldn't make that commitment. He was trying to put his life back together after this past difficult year. How could he uproot that life and live in Sweetwater—pursue Jesse?

He moved into the room and sat on the bed, patting the area next to him. When Cindy eased down beside him, he wrapped his arm about her shoulders and said, "Sweetheart, God does not grant every wish a person asks for."

"I know. Jesse told me He knows what is best and sometimes things happen differently than we want for a reason we may not know at the time. But I have to tell Him what I want. How important it is to me."

The hand about his heart tightened. He struggled to bring air into his lungs. He couldn't even tell Cindy they would be back next summer. After his discussion with Jesse yesterday, he knew that wouldn't be a good idea. She had so much to offer a man. What if she had found a husband by next summer? How could he live next door to her and want—

He shook that thought from his mind and stood. "Cindy, we need to get on the road. I want to be in Chicago by dark. Do you have everything in the car?"

With eyes glistening, she nodded.

Nick drew her to him and held her tightly against him for a long moment. "I love you, honey. We'll get back into our life in Chicago and everything will be fine."

Cindy pulled away, a tear rolling down her cheek. "No, it won't." She ran from the bedroom, pounding down the stairs.

Nick listened to her open the front door and slam it shut. The quiet in her bedroom taunted him, eroding his composure he had so carefully erected over the past twenty-four hours. He released a deep breath out through pursed lips and headed for his SUV.

Jesse stood in the middle of her kitchen, unsure of what to do. Through the window over the sink she glimpsed Nick's car in the driveway, packed and ready to go. She had to say goodbye to Cindy, but her legs wouldn't move toward the door. If she saw Cindy, she would see Nick and she didn't know if she could handle that encounter.

Nick and Cindy were leaving today. For good. She knew he wouldn't return next summer and that decision was for the best. How could she live next door to him and not dream of more? And the longer she was around him the more she would want that dream.

The doorbell chimed.

"I'll get it," Nate yelled and clamored down the stairs, the sound echoing through the house.

It would be Cindy coming to say goodbye. Jesse willed her legs to walk toward the entry hall. If she saw the little girl now, maybe she could avoid Nick. That thought prodded her to move faster.

"I prayed, too," her son said as Jesse came into the entry hall.

"It didn't work. Daddy and I are leaving in a few minutes." Cindy hung her head, her shoulders hunched.

"What didn't work?" Jesse asked, wanting to make sure the children weren't up to something else.

"Praying for Cindy to stay here."

"Oh," was all Jesse could think of to say. The pain in the children's eyes reflected her own hurt.

"Cindy. Cindy!" Nick shouted from his front yard.

"You'd better go. It sounds like your dad is getting worried." Hugging the child, Jesse kissed the top of her head. "I hope you'll write to us."

Cindy nodded. "I've got your e-mail address." Instead of leaving, she threw her arms around Jesse again and clung to her.

"Cindy, we need to go now." Nick appeared in the open door, a neutral expression on his face.

He was a master at hiding behind an expressionless facade, Jesse thought, wishing she could disappear. Now she must say goodbye to him as well.

"But, Daddy—"

"*Now,* young lady."

Cindy let Jesse go and stumped to the door, a frown firmly in place as she passed her father and headed down the steps. Nate went after her.

Jesse wanted to shout to her son not to leave her alone with Nick, but the words clogged in her throat. She cleared it and said, "Have a safe trip." Moving toward the door, she grasped the handle, ready to shut it as soon as possible.

Nick opened his mouth to say something but pressed it closed. For a second an emotion—regret?—flickered in his eyes, but quickly that bland expression descended. "Goodbye, Jesse." He pivoted and hurried toward his SUV.

Jesse watched for a couple of seconds too long, then finally closed the front door. Collapsing back against the wood, she squeezed her eyes shut to keep the tears inside. She would not cry over him. This was for the best. A relationship wouldn't have worked out between them because…

For the life of her she couldn't think of one reason it wouldn't. She knew there were reasons but her mind went blank. Her heart ruled and it bled.

Chapter Thirteen

❧

"Anyone want any more iced tea?" Jesse asked, holding up the glass pitcher.

"No, I'll float home if I have a refill. As it is I spend half my time in the bathroom." Darcy set her tall glass down on the coaster.

Zoey laughed. "That's what being pregnant does to a woman. Reduces her to checking out every rest room everywhere she goes. I should know. I've got three kids."

"That, or standing on the scales moaning about all the pounds she is gaining." Tanya took the pitcher and poured some more tea.

"True. I'm already gaining faster than I should, and I'm only three and a half months pregnant. What in the world am I going to look like in a few more months? The Goodyear blimp?"

"I got to raise three children without the wonders of being pregnant. I think I lucked out after listening to you all." Beth grabbed a chocolate chip cookie from the platter on Jesse's coffee table.

"Yeah, in a few months you won't know what to do with all your free time," Zoey said.

"I can't believe Daniel's finally graduating from high school. It's been a long battle to get to this place, but after he goes off to college in January, I'm a free woman."

Jesse sank down onto a lounge chair, tired, her heart not really into this weekly Saturday afternoon gabfest even if the four other women were her good friends. She listened to them talk about school starting, raising children and dieting, all subjects she usually commented on. But not this time.

Darcy had started this circle of friends because of Tanya's and Zoey's needs a few months back. Now Jesse found she needed their support, but wasn't sure how to ask. She'd never been good at asking for help.

Darcy cocked her head and looked at Jesse. "You're awfully quiet. What's up? Nick?"

Leave it to her best friend from high school to home in on what was eating at her, Jesse thought and said, "Yes. They've been gone a month and I still think about him every day. I'm even dreaming about him." She gestured toward her face. "Hence the tired lines."

"Did you tell him how you felt about him?"

"What do you mean?"

"Did you tell him you loved him?"

"I don't—I mean, I love Cindy and care for Nick. I—"

Darcy held up her hand. "Hold it right there. You love him, Jesse." She motioned toward her face. "Hence the tired lines."

"Tell him. How can he make a good decision about the future without all the information?" Beth picked up her glass, running her finger along its edge.

"I can't call him. I don't have his number. It's unlisted."

"You looked it up?" Tanya asked, snatching up a cookie and taking a bite.

Jesse nodded. "One night right after he left. I wanted to make sure he got home okay." That was the feeblest excuse because Cindy had e-mailed them when she had arrived.

"There are other ways of contacting him. You know where he lives. You have his e-mail address. You could call him at work. Why haven't you tried harder?" Beth took a sip of her drink, then replaced her glass on the coaster.

If her friends had said this to her two weeks ago, Jesse would have broken down and cried. But she didn't have any tears left in her. Her emotions were dried up. Where her heart beat there was emptiness. "I don't want to be hurt anymore. I made it through Mark's death. I thought I had protected myself against that kind of pain. I was wrong. Nick made me relive it all over again when he left. I only knew him for two months and I fell hard for him. Those feelings scare me."

"It means you are alive. Haven't you heard love is what makes the world go around?"

"That coming from the only married woman in the

group," Jesse said, a headache beginning to form behind her eyes.

"Hey, Zoey and Tanya are still married." The instant Darcy said those words, she clamped her hand over her mouth, her eyes wide. "I'm so sorry, Zoey and Tanya."

Zoey smiled but there was a sadness in her eyes. "I am married. That is a fact. Ignoring it won't change it. Just because my husband has disappeared, is probably dead, doesn't mean you all have to watch what you say around me. It's been a year."

Tanya finished chewing her cookie. "Even though my husband is in prison, I'll stand behind him. I made a vow to God that I would."

"We're quite a group, aren't we?" Beth shifted, uncrossing her legs.

"We are. I appreciate your advice and I will think about trying to call him. I don't think it will make any difference that I love him. We live too far apart."

"That can be changed. He could live here. You could live there." Zoey brushed her long hair behind her shoulders.

"I'm not talking about mere miles. He hasn't been able to forgive himself or his wife and without that I don't think we could ever be truly happy. His past would come between us."

"Let's pray." Beth held out her hands.

Everyone joined hands and bowed their heads.

"Dear Heavenly Father, bless this group with Your wisdom. We give You thanks for all You have done for us. Please guide us in what needs to be done and espe-

cially help Jesse through this difficult time. Amen."
Beth looked up at Jesse. "Talk to Nick. Let him know
how you feel."

As Jesse cleaned up after her friends left, she thought
back over their advice. E-mailing was out of the question—too impersonal. Should she call Nick at work? Or,
should she go to see him? Her hands trembled as she
put the dishes in the sink. If she did anything, she should
do it in person. But could she see Nick again? What if
he had moved on, didn't care? How could she face his
indifference?

"That will be all. Go home, folks." Nick closed the
file on his desk and waited until his three vice presidents
filed out of his office before he allowed the exhaustion
he felt to show.

His shoulders hunched, he collapsed back in his
chair and spun around to view the lights of Chicago.
Nighttime. He should have been home an hour ago, but
the meeting had gone over and now he wouldn't arrive before Cindy was in bed. He liked reading to her
before she went to sleep, but Boswell would in his
place. That thought didn't settle the restlessness he ex-
perienced more and more since coming home to
Chicago.

Nothing satisfied him—not even work. The only time
he felt remotely at peace was when he attended church
with Cindy. When he stepped through the sanctuary's
doors, he felt as though he wasn't alone in this world—
that God was truly with him. The first Sunday had sur-

prised him. Now he looked forward to going to church and experiencing the peace in his soul.

Nick gathered up some papers to review and stuck them in his briefcase. Quickly he headed for the elevator and the car that would be waiting for him downstairs in front of his office building.

On the short drive home he laid his head on the cushion and closed his eyes, trying to remember a night when he had gotten enough sleep. Not since Sweetwater. Not since his dreams were haunted by Jesse—by the promise her laugh brought to him. She had shown him the way back to the Lord. She had given him his life back with his daughter. What was he doing in Chicago?

When the driver stopped in front of his apartment building, Nick climbed out and hurried to the penthouse elevator. Maybe Cindy was still awake. He needed to hold his daughter. To see her smile. To chase away the demons that plagued him.

Inside his apartment that took up the whole top floor of the building, he saw the skyline of Chicago lit up with lights, the lake beyond. He didn't stop to admire the view but tossed his briefcase on the large round table in the middle of the foyer. He strode through the elegant living room with its drapes open, down the hall toward Cindy's room.

Boswell met him as he came out of his daughter's room. "I just read her a story. Even though she was fighting sleep, I believe she is still up."

"Good." Nick stepped around Boswell and peered into Cindy's room.

His daughter had slipped from between the sheets and knelt beside the bed. She folded her hands and said, "God, I almost forgot to pray to You. Please bless Daddy, Boswell, Jesse—"

Nick didn't want to interrupt his daughter while praying. He was glad she had added praying into her nightly routine. He even found himself ending his day with a prayer to the Lord. He remembered his first few awkward attempts. But Jesse had once said to him that praying was like having a conversation with the Lord. It didn't have to be fancy—just plain and simple and from the heart. After recalling that advice it had been easy for him.

"—and God, don't forget my request for a new mother. Please make sure Mommy doesn't mind. I still love her, but I want someone to make my daddy happy because he's the best daddy in the world and he deserves it. I want Jesse."

His throat constricted. He wanted Jesse, too. Why hadn't he seen what she had done for him and Cindy? Why had he run away from the best thing that had happened to him? Because he was afraid he couldn't make Jesse happy as she deserved. Because he hadn't been a good husband in his first marriage.

"Daddy, you're home!"

Nick forced his attention on his daughter, smiling and walking into her bedroom. "I couldn't let you go to sleep without saying good-night to me."

When he bent down to give her a kiss, Cindy threw her arms around his neck. "I've already had a story, but you can read me another one."

"I can, can I? Which one?"

Cindy grabbed the book that Boswell had obviously been reading from her nightstand. "This one. He read chapter five."

"So I should read the next chapter." Nick sat on the bed and let Cindy snuggle against him.

He opened the book to chapter six and began to read. Halfway through the second page he noticed that Cindy was asleep. He slipped his arm from around her shoulders and stood. After tucking her in, he grabbed Cindy's Bible and left her bedroom, glancing back at his precious daughter as he switched off the overhead light, something she liked left on until she fell asleep.

Wearily he walked into the living room and sat in a chair near the bank of floor-to-ceiling windows. He stared out into the dark night, lit with thousands of lights from the many buildings. He had some thinking to do. He could continue with his life the way it was—only half full—or he could make a change, a drastic change.

He opened the Bible and read through the story of Christ. The words of hope took root in his heart and grew as the Lord's message to His people flowed through his mind, stirring his faith that had laid dormant for so long. When he finished reading Luke's account of Jesus's life on Earth, Nick closed the book and absorbed the peace he felt. He knew what he had to do. What if Jesse rejected him? What if she had gone on with her life never giving him another thought? How could he face her disinterest?

He sighed, staring unseeing at the darkness beyond

his windows. Exhaustion clung to him like a wet blanket. His eyelids grew heavy. He closed them and leaned back, relaxing in the lounge chair. Sleep whisked him into the land of dreams....

Someone shook his arm. He heard a child's voice through the fog and tried to focus on it.

"Daddy, wake up. What are you doing out here?"

Slowly Nick opened his eyes and looked at his daughter standing at his side with her forehead creased, her eyes dark with concern.

"Are you all right?" Cindy held her Bible clasped to her chest.

He straightened in the lounge chair, blinking at the bright light streaming through the windows. "What time is it?"

"Eight."

"Eight!" He started to rise, stopped himself and settled back into the chair. He remembered the dream he'd had the night before. It was Jesse and his wedding and his daughter stood at Jesse's left while Nate stood at his right. The sense of well-being still encased him with satisfaction. The dream had confirmed what he must do if he was ever going to be happy.

He patted his lap and Cindy leaped up into it. "Honey, would you mind if I went away for a few days?"

She frowned. "Where?"

"To Sweetwater."

"I want to go."

"If all goes well, you'll be going back to Sweetwater permanently. I'm going to ask Jesse if she will marry me."

Cindy didn't say anything for a good minute, then she let out a holler that Nick was sure they heard on the street below. This was the right decision. He knew it in his heart.

"I'm sorry, Mr. Blackburn is out of the office for the next few days. May I take a message?"

Jesse sank down onto the chair by the phone. "Yes, tell him—no, I'll call back later." She hung up, disappointed and relieved at the same time.

Wiping the perspiration from her brow, she thought about the wisdom of telling him how she felt over the phone. Maybe she should go to Chicago and see him in person? It had taken her several days since meeting with her friends on Saturday even to get the courage up to make the call to his office.

Lord, help me. I don't know what to do.

She heard the front door opening and closing. Nate yelled he was home and then the sound of him charging up the stairs floated to her. Still she couldn't decide how to proceed with Nick. She chewed on her bottom lip and stared at the floor as though the tiles had an answer written on them.

Someone cleared his throat. Jesse looked up, her heart hammering against her rib cage. Nick.

Frozen, she stared at him as hard as she had the floor. Was he a mirage?

Then he moved farther into the kitchen, a smile deep in his eyes. "Hello, Jesse."

His words came to her as though they were spoken

to her from afar. Still she couldn't move. What was happening didn't seem real.

"Jesse?" Concern darkened his gaze.

She blinked, breaking the trancelike state she was in. She surged to her feet, words tumbling through her mind. "Nick, what are you doing here? I just called your office and they said you were gone for a few days."

"I am gone. I'm here." His mouth lifted in a lopsided grin, humor lighting his eyes.

"I mean—I—" The words were gone as she peered at his handsome face—a face she had seen many times over the past month in her dreams.

"You called my office? Why?"

With three strides he was only a foot from her, so close she could reach out and touch him. Feeling weak, she backed up against the desk, clutching its edge to keep her from collapsing. "Why are you here?"

"I couldn't stay away any longer."

"Why?" Her heart increased its beat, so rapidly that she kept her grip on the desk. She still couldn't believe he was here in her house in Sweetwater.

"It's simple. I love you, Jesse Bradshaw. I have for quite some time, but have been too much of a fool to do something about it."

She collapsed back on the desk, her legs trembling. "You love me?"

He clasped her arms. "Yes. I love you. Now will you tell me why you were calling my office? Is something wrong?"

She reached up to touch his face, to trace his mouth.

"I didn't have your private home number and I needed to talk to you so I tried your office."

"Why did you need to talk with me?" Nick cuddled closer, bringing her flat against him.

She drew in a deep breath of his distinctive scent of lime and relished it. "I felt I should tell you how I felt about you."

He brushed his lips across hers and whispered, "And how do you feel about me?"

She framed his face and looked deep into his eyes. "I love you, Nick Blackburn, with all my heart. I didn't make that clear to you before you left. I should have. You need all the facts to make the best decision."

"I agree." He laid his forehead against hers, love shining in his eyes. "I'm a little slow when it comes to my emotions, but I finally figured out that just because I wasn't a success at my first marriage, I shouldn't doom myself to loneliness, especially when I have a wonderful woman like you to love and who loves me."

"Have you forgiven yourself and Brenda?"

"Last night I listened to my daughter pray to God asking for a new mother. But she also told God how much she loved her mother and to make sure she didn't mind she wanted a new one. That made me start thinking. Even though Brenda wasn't the right wife for me, she gave me a beautiful daughter and she loved Cindy. She was a good mother at least. So how can I hate someone who gave me Cindy?"

"And yourself?"

"If God can forgive me, then I can forgive myself."

"Oh, Nick." Jesse wound her arms around him and pulled him toward her.

His mouth claimed hers in a deep kiss that rocked her to her soul. Sensations she had thought she would never experience again after Mark's death flooded her.

"Do you two have to do that?"

Nick jerked back. Jesse looked toward the doorway to find her son standing there with a toy sailboat in his arms.

"Nate Bradshaw, were you eavesdropping?"

"I waited and waited. Finally I decided to come see if you two had made up. I want to show Nick the new sailboat I made. I thought we could sail it on the lake."

"Sure. Can you give me a minute with your mom?"

"Are you moving back here?" Nate asked as he headed for the back door.

"I hope so."

"You are?" Jesse asked, her surprise slipping out, suddenly remembering that barrier to their relationship.

Nick glanced at Nate who was still in the kitchen, then turned toward Jesse. "Yes, if you'll agree to marry me. I can run Blackburn Industries from here. Besides, I have decided to cut back on working so much." He took her into his arms again. "I want to devote my time to my new family."

"Mom, tell him yes so we can go to the lake and sail my boat."

Jesse laughed. "Yes, I'll marry you."

Her son's shout of joy filled the kitchen as Nick kissed her so thoroughly that her toes curled.

Epilogue

"Do I look all right?"

Jesse fixed the pink satin bow in Cindy's hair, then stepped back to appraise her maid of honor. "You look perfect, honey."

The child took her bouquet of pink roses and clasped them in front of her. "You're so beautiful, Jesse."

Her throat tight, Jesse said, "Thank you."

In the mirror she saw herself as Cindy did, wearing a pale pink silk suit with pink pearl buttons on the jacket and a straight skirt that fell to just below her knees. She picked up her bouquet of white orchids tied together with a pink bow.

"Are you ready?" Jesse asked, stepping into her two-inch high heels that had been dyed to match her suit.

With a nod Cindy led the way to the sanctuary where Nick and Gramps would be standing with Reverend Collins. From the back of the church Jesse surveyed the small gathering of friends and family. Nate, dressed in a black suit with a gray tie, offered her his arm to walk her down the aisle. A few stray strands of his hair stuck out and Jesse took a moment to brush them into place.

He squirmed. "Mom, Nick's waiting!"

"I know. A few extra seconds won't make a difference. He isn't going anywhere."

When Nate's hair was tamed, Jesse nodded to the organist to begin the wedding march and she and her son started down the aisle following Cindy. Jesse smiled at her circle of friends in the front pew. Darcy sat between Joshua and Sean while Zoey was holding baby Tara between her two other children, Mandy and Blake. Beth took up one end of the pew with Tanya at the other end. Crystal was in her wheelchair next to Tanya. Everyone's expressions reflected the joy Jesse was feeling as she walked toward the man she loved, toward her new life with Nick.

The sunlight streamed through the round window above the altar and shone on the cross that hung from the ceiling. Jesse looked heavenward. *Thank you, God, for bringing me Nick and Cindy. Thank You for giving me a second chance at love.*

Jesse stopped next to Nick and took his hand as they faced the reverend. Together, a couple, a family.

Reverend Collins spoke of love and marriage, but all Jesse could see or hear were Nick's face and his words as he repeated his vows. Her world centered around him and her family.

When the wedding ceremony was over, instead of

leaving the sanctuary, Jesse and Nick greeted their friends who surrounded them with their well wishes.

In the midst of people Cindy tugged on Jesse's arm to get her attention.

"What's wrong, sweetie?"

"Can I call you Mom now?"

Jesse hugged Cindy to her, a sudden well of tears misting her eyes. "I would be honored to be your mother."

* * * * *

Look for Beth's story in LIGHT IN THE STORM,
coming in April 2005
only from Margaret Daley
and Steeple Hill Love Inspired.

Dear Reader,

The story of Jesse and Nick in *A Mother for Cindy* came easily to me. It seemed to flow from my thoughts to the written page. The story is about a lonely man who finds his way back to God. There are times in people's lives when they doubt the Lord, often when something difficult has happened to test them. Sadly some turn away and never find their way back to the Lord. Others are lucky and have a special person to show them the importance of God's love and power. They come back to God a richer person, for their journey strengthens them.

I love hearing from my readers. You can contact me at P.O. Box 2074, Tulsa, OK 74101 or MDaley50@aol.com.

May God bless you,

Margaret Daley